CAPE MAY GLITTER

CLAUDIA VANCE

CHAPTER ONE

Margaret swatted some bugs out of her face as she placed a few bouquets of sunflowers in a bucket of water. As she turned around, she nearly stumbled on a basket of tomatoes sitting on the ground but managed to grab ahold of Dave's arm to steady herself.

"You OK?" Dave asked with a slight chuckle while wrapping his other arm around her waist.

Margaret nodded in thought. "I am. I think I'm just a little too excited," she said, taking a step back to get a full view of the new farm stand. "I still can't believe you built *this* within weeks."

Dave rubbed his chin as the cicadas became louder and louder around them. "It worked out perfectly. My brother had spare time to help, as well as some guys from Pinetree Wildlife Refuge. Then Dale, Chris, and Greg stopped by—mostly to have a drink and talk, but they nailed a board or two," he said with a smile.

Margaret shook her head in disbelief. "It's probably the most gorgeous farm stand I've ever seen. It looks like a tiny house. I mean, you've added windows, blue shutters, and white wood siding," she said while walking over to a window and peering in.

Dave shrugged. "I wanted to make it unique to us," he said while sitting down in one of the teal rocking chairs he'd placed on a cement patio in front of the stand.

Margaret smiled and looked up at the large oak tree shading them from the scorching August sun above. Then she gazed at the stone pathway Dave had put in that led from the street to the stand. "So much work went into this. I'm just … impressed."

Dave blushed then stood up and walked inside the farm stand with Margaret following behind. "Now, I built this extra counter for the money box and bags for the customer."

Margaret nodded. "That will work great since we're doing the honor system. They can leave their payment in the locked box and bag their items before leaving."

"Exactly," Dave said while bending down to pick up the basket of red Roma tomatoes Margaret had nearly tripped on earlier. "Where should I put this?"

Margaret scanned the stand. "Gosh, we're fully stocked, aren't we? I have to fit them in somewhere. How about there?" she said, pointing next to a basket of onions

The little stand was chock-full of freshly picked home-grown garden produce: zucchini, tomatoes in every color and size, cucumbers, peppers, eggplants. You name it. Also offered were colorful zinnia, celosia, bells of Ireland, and sunflower bouquets. White string lights had been strung from corner to corner across the ceiling, and sweet little vintage teacups and saucers, books, and trinkets that Margaret had thrifted sat nestled in between all of it both for decoration and to buy.

Dave walked to the oak tree, grabbed the six-foot ladder leaning against it, and stood it up in the front of the stand.

"What are you doing?" Margaret asked as she watched him walk back inside the farm stand.

Dave kneeled down and pulled out a wooden slab from

under the counter then carried it to the ladder. "I made a sign."

Margaret stared at the large wooden slab with eye hooks drilled into it. "Really? But we haven't come up with a name."

Dave smiled. "We did, remember? Last week you came up with something great," he said while climbing up the ladder and hanging the sign on the hooks.

Margaret shook her head as she racked her brain, not remembering any of it, but as she saw the writing on the sign, it came back to her. *The Beach House Market.*

"You mentioned that the farm stand reminded you of a little beach house, and it stuck with me," Dave said as he hopped off the ladder and folded it up while staring up at the sign.

Margaret smiled. "I can't believe you remembered that. I didn't think you were listening."

Dave smirked. "I'm always listening."

"It's perfect," Margaret said as she looked at the white cursive writing on the sign.

"Liz made it in her garage studio. We kept it a surprise," Dave said with a wink.

Margaret smiled then looked out towards the quiet road, noticing only a bicyclist riding by. "Do you really think there's a demand for another farm market in West Cape May? I mean, there're already a bunch. Not to mention, how will they find us? We're on a back road, not one of the main roads everyone comes into town on."

Dave put his arm around Margaret's shoulders. "Look, right now, we're really doing this for us. We've wanted our own little stand since we put that one on Liz and Greg's property. It brings us joy. If it's successful, great. If it's not, then we'll figure something out."

Margaret nodded and leaned her head on Dave's shoulder. "You're right. Plus, maybe we can put a sign at the end of our street. There's so much produce and flowers in the market right now, I'd hate to see it go to waste."

Harper and Abby came walking out in bare feet from the house towards them, each holding a paper bag.

"What are you two up to?" Margaret asked as they approached.

"We're setting up the fairy garden," Harper said as she started emptying her bag onto the grass. Abby did the same. Out poured miniature mushrooms, foxes, chairs, watering cans, gnomes, tiny houses, and perfectly smooth gray rocks.

Margaret smiled. "That's a great idea. Where should it go?" she asked, eyeing the many different potential spots around the property.

"How about by the tree? That seems like the perfect place for fairies to live," Abby said, placing her items back into her bag. Harper did the same, and they headed towards the oak on a mission.

Margaret looked at her watch. "I have to get over to the Seahorse Inn. Paul will probably be here in about a half hour to pick up the girls. Are you OK to handle that?"

Dave glanced at the girls, who were happily setting up their fairy garden. "I'll be fine. I'll even help them find their shoes before he gets here."

Margaret laughed then kissed Dave on the cheek. "Perfect. I won't be too long. We've just got a lot going on, and I need to be at the Seahorse to help out."

"You're hosting that women's retreat, right?" Dave asked.

Margaret nodded. "Indeed we are, and it's our first time. It sold out in two days. Word must have spread fast. We have women coming from all over. Who knew there was such a demand for this type of thing for women over fifty."

"There's an age requirement?" Dave asked, confused.

"There is," Margaret said as she walked towards the girls, noticing they had already set up the perfect fairy garden within minutes. "I guess you didn't need my help, huh?"

Abby made a face. "Your help? I don't need your help, Mom." Harper nodded in agreement.

Margaret glanced at Dave and shrugged. "Phew. That's a relief. I guess they won't be needing help with any homework this year either."

Harper and Abby both rolled their eyes while Dave and Margaret nudged each other, laughing.

* * *

"OK, ladies. Sorry I'm late. We were finishing the final touches on the farm stand. What did I miss?" Margaret asked as she set her purse on the island counter then took a seat at the packed kitchen table between Liz and Dolly. In the other seats were Kim, Irene, Jackie, and Bonnie.

Dolly lowered her glasses. "We'd just started. So, I'll start from the beginning, but first, help yourself to some new recipes we're trying out. Blueberry iced tea and apricot scones."

Liz reached to the center of the table, picking up a clear glass pitcher of blue iced tea, while Irene placed a scone on a small plate and handed it across the table to Margaret.

After pouring the iced tea into an empty glass on the table, Liz abruptly got up. "Hold on. It needs a garnish," she said while walking to the fridge. She came back with a small skewer of fresh blueberries and placed it on the rim of the glass. "OK, it's ready."

Margaret smiled as she took a sip and looked around at the ladies, all watching her with anticipation. "Wow. Just wow. What's in this?"

Jackie spoke up. "It's homemade blueberry juice with steeped black tea. It's great, isn't it?"

Margaret widened her eyes as she took another sip. "It's the best iced tea I've ever had."

Jackie clapped. "I'm so glad you like it. We're thinking it will be a great summer refreshment for the women's retreat."

5

Dolly cleared her throat. "About that. Let's get back to discussing the retreat."

Everyone quieted down.

Dolly looked around the table. "This is our first time hosting a women's retreat at the Seahorse Inn. We sold all the open spots in two days. As you already know, it's for women fifty and over only—"

Liz interrupted. "Why fifty?"

Dolly took off her glasses. "Well, I personally saw a need for it. Kim and I joined a travel group earlier this year that headed to Scotland. I guess we didn't research it enough, because little did we know, we were the oldest ones there, and I'm not talking about a ten-year difference. I'm talking twenty, thirty, even forty years."

Kim cut in. "Now, we don't have an issue with being around younger age groups, but in this instance, it wasn't ideal. We're in our sixties. Our idea of a good time on vacation can be starkly different from a twenty-five-year-old's. We, essentially, felt alienated from everyone else in this small travel group. Luckily, we had each other."

Dolly nodded. "We still made the most of the trip, but while the younger folk were out clubbing until the wee hours of the morning, Kim and I were in bed. While they all slept in, Kim and I caught beautiful sunrises, ate breakfast, and hung out with the local tour guide."

Kim laughed. "It was actually quite nice because we got our own personal tour of the area while everyone else slept through it. The show had to go on."

Bonnie cocked her head to the side in confusion. "They just slept through the tour? The tour they signed up and paid for?"

Dolly nodded. "You betcha. I mean, if they were fine with it, great, but Kim and I were hoping to meet up with like-minded ladies, and it was anything but that. We felt like two old grandmothers with absolutely nothing in common with the rest of the group."

Irene shook her head. "That should all be disclosed before anyone signs up and pays for something like that."

Dolly clasped her hands together. "And that's why we wanted to put a minimum age requirement for this retreat."

Margaret took a bite of her scone and swallowed. "There definitely was a need for it. It sold out so quickly."

Kim smiled. "We're glad you and Liz were on board with our idea. This is very exciting for us."

Dolly opened her notebook. "So, nine ladies in total are coming. All solo. All with their own rooms for ten days. A handful are local, and the rest are coming from places like Florida, Ohio, Massachusetts, and even one from Kansas and another from Texas. Barring no flight delays, they should all be arriving Sunday afternoon."

Bonnie smiled. "This is so exciting for some reason. It feels like we're all about to go on this women's retreat too."

Dolly smirked. "That might have been part of my plan. We never got to make any connections during the Scotland trip, so maybe we can do it here in Cape May."

Kim slid Dolly's notebook towards herself. "Let's go over the itinerary we've put together. For some of it, we may have to go by the seat of our pants—like for instance, if there's bad weather—but overall, I think it's great."

Liz nodded. "And we were pretty resourceful, so it kept the cost of the retreat down."

"Exactly," Kim said as she slid her finger down the page she was staring at. "We'll be doing our normal tea-and-cookies hour, wine-and-cheese hour, and brunch. We have a day at Liz and Greg's pool since the pool here at the Seahorse is still being fixed. We have a boating adventure on the Blue Heron Birding boat and dinners at Donna's Restaurant, Heirloom, and other Cape May establishments planned and reserved."

"Don't forget the garden tour at our place," Margaret added in.

Dolly nodded. "It's come together quite nicely. We haven't even gone over all the plans, and there is so much already. We do want this retreat to feel relaxing but also exciting and inspiring. We want everyone to feel welcome, and we certainly want to make sure the group is enjoying themselves."

Irene stood up abruptly from her seat. "I forgot to turn the oven on for the zucchini bread."

Jackie laughed. "The loaf has just been sitting in the oven this whole time?"

Irene rolled her eyes. "Yes. Let's hope I remember to do it this week when the guests are here."

Everyone laughed.

Bonnie refilled her iced tea glass. "Let's not forget about the basement for the movie theater experience."

Dolly grabbed her notebook back from Kim. "Oh, it's already on the list somewhere on here. We also have tickets for a show at the Cape May Movie Theater."

Margaret nodded. "How are we on laundry and cleaning? Is there more to be done?"

Irene shook her head. "All taken care of. We had some guests leave a little early yesterday, which let us get that cleaned a lot quicker."

"How about food shopping?" Liz asked.

"Also taken care of. Of course, we'll need to do more throughout the week, but we should be good for the first few days," Dolly said.

"So we're set then?" Margaret asked as she stood up to bring her empty plate and glass to the dishwasher.

"We're more than ready," Dolly said as she closed her notebook.

Margaret grabbed her purse. "Perfect. I want to get back to the Beach House Market to add a few more things."

Jackie smiled. "You named it 'The Beach House Market'? I love that."

Margaret glanced at Liz and smiled. "Apparently, Dave says I came up with the name, and Liz made the sign, unbeknownst to me. You all will have to come by. It's the most darling little market you ever saw."

Liz nodded. "It really is. You'll see how the name fits the aesthetic perfectly. It was fun making the sign in my garage workshop."

Margaret tapped Liz on the shoulder and smiled. "I may have to commission you to make me a few furniture pieces for inside of it."

CHAPTER TWO

The next morning, Dave and Margaret headed out to the Beach House Market with their coffees in hand.

Margaret yawned as the morning sun stretched slowly across the green lawn. "I'm not expecting anything to have sold, but I am expecting to see a couple of rotted vegetables with this heat we've been having."

Dave nodded as they approached the stand, and then they both stopped in their tracks, staring.

Margaret lifted her sunglasses to the top of her head. "Do you see what I see?"

Dave squinted his eyes. "I'm seeing a lot of missing flowers and produce."

Margaret scratched her head. "There's no way all of this sold in less than twenty-four hours. We haven't even spread word that we're open."

Dave shrugged. "Well, either we got lucky or the squirrels and chipmunks did."

They both rushed over to the money box with excitement building.

"You do the honors," Margaret said as she felt herself getting impatient.

Dave pulled a key out of his pocket, unlocked the padlock on the money box, then opened it. He peered inside. "Well, that's a surprise."

"What is?" Margaret asked as she moved in to take a peek inside.

Dave pulled out a handful of cash and a few personal checks. "Looks like we beat out the squirrels 1–0."

Margaret squealed with glee and jumped up and down, clapping. "I can't believe it! We've had our very first customers."

Dave smiled as he counted the money out. "There's about a hundred dollars here."

Margaret felt her heart leap as she walked around the market. "What do you think they bought? We should probably head to the garden and replace it."

Dave pointed to the flower bouquets. "Looks like a bunch of the sunflowers and zinnias are gone."

Margaret nodded then pointed to the produce table. "And a lot of the slicer tomatoes, jalapeños, and eggplants. I'm going to head up to the garden and pick some more to bring down."

"Good idea. I'll join," Dave said as he finished his coffee and set his mug down on the counter.

Five minutes later, Margaret was cutting sunflower stalks while Dave was across the yard, picking tomatoes. She cut her last stalk and held the bundled flowers in her hand as she headed towards Dave.

"Dave, do you think our friends and family were the customers we had?" Margaret asked, starting to grow skeptical about their early success.

Dave picked a red Early Girl tomato and held it up to the sun to see the perfection, then looked back at Margaret. "Gosh, I hope not. They can get all of this for free, and they know that. Did they even know we had stocked and opened the stand?"

Margaret nodded. "They did. They all knew yesterday was

going to be opening day. It's starting to make more sense now. You know how secretly supportive Liz and Greg like to be sometimes."

Dave shrugged as he started walking with Margaret back towards the market with their tomatoes and flowers. "Well, text them. See if it was any of them. That'll clear it up."

Margaret shook her head. "Maybe, but I feel like they won't admit to it. Is it horrible that I wish it wasn't them? I was really hopeful that we could have a thriving little business here."

"I get it. I really do," Dave said as they walked into their market and started placing the flowers into the buckets of water and putting the tomatoes on the counter. "I think, though, that we've got something unique and fun here that sets us apart. Plus, we're growing the items right up the way. It's a family operation, and people like to support small businesses like this. Give it some time."

"You're right," Margaret said as she forced a hopeful smile.

Dave set the last tomato down then glanced at his phone after a message popped up. "Another cancellation."

Margaret widened her eyes. "Please tell me you're not talking about the bay house rental."

Dave nodded and put his phone back in his pocket. "Talk about last minute. The new renters were supposed to check in today around three, and I'm getting this cancellation at 8 a.m.? I guess it's good we still get the deposit and cancellation fee money."

"This is the third last-minute cancellation this summer. What is going on?" Margaret asked, feeling bewildered.

"Beats me. It is getting to be very inconvenient, though. We could have rented this week out to another family. Now, there's not any time. Same goes for those other cancellations," Dave said as he stepped out of the market and looked out towards a car passing by on the road.

"We need to set more rules or increase the cancellation

charge to prevent this from happening in the future," Margaret said as she picked up their empty coffee mugs off the counter.

"Well, the current renters should be out soon. I'm going to head over there shortly to clean. I figure I'll get ahead of the game, even if there aren't any new renters coming this week," Dave said as he put his hand on the small of Margaret's back. They headed back toward the house.

"I feel bad that I can't help, but I told the ladies I'd bake pies for the women's retreat. It's going to be an entire day of baking. Though ... I may be able to spend an hour at the bay house cleaning before I pick the girls up from Paul's later," Margaret said as they walked up the steps to the front porch.

Dave put his arm around her shoulders and kissed her cheek. "I've got this, dear. It's just the usual: vacuuming, sweeping, emptying the dishwasher, wiping surfaces, cleaning the bathroom, and doing laundry. It will only take about two hours max since the renters bring their own bed linens."

They walked inside into the cool house, and Margaret set the coffee mugs down on the dining room table then turned to Dave. "I feel like you never have a moment's rest. You work all week at Pinetree, you just finished building this amazing farm stand and stocked it with me, and now you have to go clean our rental. Why don't you wait and we can do it together one day this week? We have time."

Dave shook his head. "I don't mind, really. I usually put on some eighties music and get in my zone. Plus, I want to stop by and see how Chris and Sarah are making out," he said, turning to shut the open front door. "Oh, look at that. A car is driving slowly by the market. Maybe we'll catch a customer in the act."

Margaret walked towards Dave and peered out of the front door, waiting to see if the passing car would stop. It slowed down but then hit the accelerator and drove right past the market. Her heart sank a little. "I'm too impatient for this. I'm about ready to stand on the corner with a sign pointing up our street," she said with a chuckle.

Dave laughed. "You are something, you know that?"

* * *

"Chris, pivot it to the left so it fits next to the dresser," Sarah said as they walked towards the moving truck, each holding one end of the large couch.

Chris pivoted the couch and then hoisted his end into the truck. "OK, I've got it from here," he said as he hopped into the truck and pulled the couch to the back of it.

"Impressive," Sarah said as she watched Chris's bicep muscles flex while positioning the couch next to the dresser.

Just then, a truck slowly passed them.

"Hey, you two!" Dave yelled out of the passenger window as he pulled into the driveway next door. He then got out of his truck and walked over to Chris and Sarah, who were taking a much-needed water break. "Well, this is giving me a little déjà vu. I remember when I was moving into our house next door, and here you guys are moving out."

Sarah smiled as she wiped some sweat off her forehead with the back of her arm. "It's crazy, isn't it? Feels like yesterday. I never thought Chris would ever want to sell this place—"

Chris cut in. "Well, that time has come. I've always wanted a place with my own boat slip, and the perfect place for us on the harbor suddenly became available. It's gorgeous. Wait until you see it, Dave."

"I'm looking forward to it. As soon as you're moved in, have us over. We'll bring the drinks," Dave said with a smile.

The smile on Chris's face faded as he looked towards Dave and Margaret's bay house. "Yeah … about drinks …"

Dave shifted his eyes. "What's up?"

Chris sighed. "The last renters you had were *something*. They just left a little bit ago."

"Looking very hungover," Sarah said with a hesitant chuckle.

"Oh?" Dave asked. "Were they loud?"

Chris nodded. "Very loud, and extremely obnoxious. All night they had music blasting, right up until 4 a.m. Lots of people were coming and going. They had some kind of huge party. I called you but never heard back."

Dave widened his eyes in disbelief. "You're kidding. How were they the rest of the week?"

Sarah shrugged. "We weren't home a lot of the week as we were working and then out in the evenings shopping for furniture for the new place, but I did hear from Tina next door that they had seen beer cans thrown all over the lawn. The renters must have cleaned up, though."

Dave stared at his bay house. "Our next renters cancelled last minute, and I'm here to clean the place. I have to say, I'm a little nervous to go in there."

"I don't blame you. Let us know if you need anything," Chris said as he finished his drink and set it on the ground by the truck.

Dave shook his head. "I appreciate it, but I should be helping you two right now, not vice versa. Moving out of a house is a lot more work than doing a little light cleaning. I'll catch up with you two later," Dave said as he pulled out his house key and made his way to the front door.

Chris and Sarah watched, feeling slight dread for the poor guy.

Dave walked onto the porch, taking note that nothing seemed out of place. He nodded to himself as he unlocked the front door. "So far so good."

He opened the door and was immediately overcome by six or seven flies trying to find their way out of the house. He ducked away from them when he caught a whiff of something awful.

As he shut the front door behind him, he looked around the living room, noticing the couch cushions were scattered all over the room, a painting on the wall hung completely lopsided, and the coffee table was full of empty beer and soda cans. His heart sank in his chest as he entered the dining room in disbelief. Here was where the awful smell and the flies were coming from. Rotting bananas, half-eaten bags of chips, and five greasy boxes of pizza.

Dave opened one of the boxes, seeing three old slices still sat inside. He closed it and pulled out his phone to call Margaret as he walked into the kitchen, when his feet started sticking to the floor with each step.

"Hey!" Margaret answered.

Dave gulped. "I hate to bother you while you're working, but we have a bit of a situation at the bay house."

"What?" Margaret asked as she stopped in her tracks.

"The place is completely trashed. Food and empty cans are everywhere. The floor is full of sticky beer, and apparently, I missed a call from Chris telling me that there was a loud party with a lot of people until the wee hours of the morning last night," Dave said as he stared at a sink piled high with dirty dishes. "I haven't even gone in the bathroom or bedrooms yet. I'm afraid to."

"This is insane. We will probably have to keep the cleaning deposit," Margaret said as she started to feel anxiety creep up within her.

Dave nodded as he walked into one of the bedrooms, noticing the blinds were completely broken and the furniture had been rearranged. "They pushed the queen bed up against the wall and scratched the wood flooring in the process," he said, bending down to inspect it closer.

"I'm honestly heartbroken this has happened. Between this and the cancellations, it's been a stressful summer with this rental. I'll be over to clean with you when I leave the Seahorse in a little bit," Margaret said as she paced back and forth.

Dave walked into the bathroom. "Well, aside from a torn shower curtain, it looks like they kept the bathroom relatively clean." He abruptly stopped. "Nope, I spoke too soon. There are marks on the wall, and there's sand all over the bottom of the shower. That's going to clog our pipes. Let me call you back. This is going to take more than a day to clean, even with the two of us. We'll figure something out for this week. I'm going to check out the yard next." They said their goodbyes and hung up.

Out in the yard was a broken pop-up tent, many lawn chairs strewn about, and even more empty beer cans everywhere.

"We have a recycling bin right here by the back door. They couldn't be bothered to clean up after themselves?" Dave asked out loud to nobody.

"Oh, good, you're here," a voice said behind the fence to Dave.

"James? Is that you?"

James peeked over the fence directly behind Dave's house. "Yes, we called the cops on your last renters. I think a few of us did. They kept my wife and me up all night. Our grandchildren slept through it, thankfully."

Dave shook his head. "James, I'm so sorry. We try to properly vet our renters, and we have rules that state no parties or loud music after ten. They trashed our place. You should see it. It looks like a bunch of frat boys stayed here. It's going to take us a while to clean it all up."

James nodded. "I'm sorry to hear that. They were definitely adults. We saw them. I guess some people just never grow up."

Dave picked up an empty can and tossed it into the recycling bin and suddenly started to question if renting out the bay house was worth it.

CHAPTER THREE

"They're here. They're here!" Dolly yelled as she watched from the window as a couple rental cars pulled into the Seahorse's driveway.

Kim looked at her watch. "Three o'clock. Right on the dot. I'm guessing the rest of them will trickle in."

"Here comes the rest of them," Dolly said as some cars pulled up on the street, dropping the passengers off.

Liz and Margaret walked into the foyer from the kitchen. "We have everything ready for tea hour once they finish getting settled in their rooms," Liz said while brushing her hands on her apron.

Margaret opened the front door to the nine ladies with suitcases. "Welcome to the Seahorse Inn, everyone! I'm guessing you're all here for the women's retreat. Come in. Come in! I'm Margaret," she said as the ladies said their hellos and walked inside.

Liz waved. "I'm Liz, and this is Dolly and Kim. You'll meet Irene, Jackie, and Bonnie tomorrow."

"It's crazy how you all arrived right at 3 p.m. I was positive someone would have a flight delay or hit traffic on the way here," Dolly said.

One of the ladies laughed as she set her suitcase down. "My flight actually landed a half hour early, but my Uber driver got lost on the way here. He had us driving around Stone Harbor instead of Cape May. I think he put in the wrong address."

Margaret smiled. "You got a nice little detour. Stone Harbor is great." She turned to the rest of the group. "I'm sure a lot of you probably need to use the bathroom and want to freshen up. Follow me, and I'll show you to your rooms," she said as she started going up the steps with the ladies following behind.

Thirty minutes later, all nine of the women were on the front porch, mingling during tea hour, which consisted of a pitcher of blueberry iced tea and regular black tea, as well as homemade scones and other pastries. The porch stretched around the inn and had large green ferns hanging from it.

Dolly set her glass of tea down and got everyone's attention. "We want to welcome you all to our first retreat for women over fifty. Kim and I had the idea for this after we ended up in a travel group with mostly twenty- and thirty-year-olds, unbeknownst to us."

Kim stood up from her seat. "We thought it would be a good idea for everyone to get to know each other. So why don't you all tell us your name, a little about yourself, and why you chose to be here."

A gorgeous woman with red hair held her hand up. "I'll go first if that's OK."

Kim smiled, delighted that someone had volunteered. "Great. Thank you for taking the lead."

"I'm Maggie. Sixty-two years old. I'm a realtor from Massachusetts with two adult children and four grandkids. I'm newly divorced after being in an unhappy marriage for way too long, and this seemed like the perfect opportunity to get away. Everyone always made it seem like life gets boring after you turn sixty, but I must say, it's been more exciting than ever. I feel like a new person; like life is beginning again."

Another woman spoke up. "Nice to meet you, Maggie. I love that you're taking life by the horns." She then turned to everyone else. "I'm Samantha. I'm from Kansas, born and raised. I'm fifty-five and was a stay-at-home mom for many years before going back to school to become a paralegal. My dear husband of thirty years passed away unexpectedly last year. He was my travel partner, and we had so many more adventures planned for the coming years, especially after retirement. It turned my world upside down. It's taken a lot for me to come out of my shell, but I finally feel ready to travel again. I'm glad to be here."

"And we're glad to have you," Margaret said as she raised her glass of tea.

"Hi, I'm Susan," a woman with short brown hair said. "I'm from Texas, as you can tell by my accent. I'm fifty-two, and I teach high school math. I, too, am divorced after being in a not-so-great marriage for years. The problem is my ex-husband turned our kids against me. They won't speak to me, so we've been estranged for a couple years. It's been rough, but I've finally realized I need to start taking care of myself, and that includes getting away to Cape May, New Jersey with all you lovely ladies."

Dolly felt tears welling up in her eyes. This retreat was turning into much more than a little getaway for women over fifty. These were women who truly needed this in their life. "Anyone want to go next?" she asked as she looked around at the remaining women.

"Me," a soft voice said from a rocking chair in the back. "Hi, everyone. I'm Chrissy. I'm not divorced or widowed. I'm actually in a happy marriage. The only problem is I love to travel and my husband doesn't. We've done some traveling together, but nothing like what I've always envisioned for myself. I've finally decided to start traveling without him, and he's very supportive of it. Oh yeah, I'm seventy. I guess I'm one of the oldest here."

"Oldest? Not quite," another woman with long black hair and multiple bangles on her wrist said with a chuckle. "I'm seventy-three. Never got married, never had kids, and I've been traveling everywhere since my twenties. I've always wanted to see Cape May, and this retreat gave me a good reason to get here. Oh yeah, I'm Tonya," she said as she waved and all of the bangles clinked together.

Margaret leaned closer to whisper in Liz's ear, "She's spunky. I like her."

Liz quietly chuckled. "She is, and these other women are so inspiring. For some, it took a lot to even get here."

A woman with long blond hair spoke up. "Hi, I'm Becky. I'm from New Jersey. It took me about an hour and a half to get here, which to me is practically local," she said with a smile. "Anyway, I'm newly retired after working as a nurse for years, and I'm ready to start finally having some real adventures. I've taken care of people my whole life, and now I just want to focus on myself. Is that selfish?"

"Absolutely not. Don't be silly!" another woman said from the back. "I'm Darlene, everyone. I'm also from New Jersey, but near Princeton. I'm fifty-five and work as a lawyer. I absolutely love Cape May and needed a reason to get here … but really, if you don't mind me getting personal, my husband of twenty-five years left me when I was diagnosed with cancer five years ago. I beat it, and have been in remission since, but it was a very low point in my life. Since then, I've been living every day as though it was a gift. I've even started dating someone great for a few weeks now. Not sure where that's going, but it's exciting. I'm just glad to be here. It seems we have all overcome some obstacles to get us here at this point."

"You certainly have," Kim said as she held her glass of tea up for a toast. All the ladies toasted with her. "We have two more people to go …"

A lady wearing a colorful Lilly Pulitzer dress and pink high heels raised her glass again. "I'm Kristen. I'm sixty-five, newly retired, and newly divorced. I owned and ran a cupcake shop for many years and still bake for some clients on the side here and there. However, one of my younger employees had an affair with my husband, which led to our divorce. It completely blindsided me, causing this confident woman to suddenly doubt her appearance and worth. It's hard to explain unless you've experienced it. Since then, I've traveled everywhere, taking trips to Bali, Peru, France, and Iceland. I'm on a roll, and I'm not stopping anytime soon. It'd be nice to find love again, but if it doesn't happen, I'm totally OK with living my happy life the way it is."

The last woman clapped her hands. "You all are inspiring me so much. You don't even know. I'm Maryanne. I'm newly widowed and am navigating life alone for the first time ever. It was always my husband and me. We never had kids, and I don't have siblings. I worked as a postal carrier for years, and am now retired, and I've decided that I need to start getting out in the world and making connections with other people. This is my first go at it, and by golly, I'm proud of myself for coming this far."

Margaret, Liz, Dolly, and Kim wiped tears from their eyes.

"I don't remember the last time I felt this emotional over our guests," Margaret said while walking around and giving everyone a hug.

"Same. I'm getting a tissue," Dolly said as she rushed inside.

Kim called after Dolly, "Bring me a tissue, too."

"You might as well bring the whole box," Liz called out with a chuckle.

* * *

Judy leaned on the counter, looking at the clock ticking in the corner as easy listening music played over the speakers. She reached down to pull a book out of her purse when her phone rang.

"Barb, thank goodness you called," Judy answered, walking around the little store.

"Why do you say that?" Barb asked with a chuckle.

Judy stopped to look at a pair of earrings made of blue sea glass. "I just started this part-time job at a little jewelry store on Sunset Boulevard. I've been here for four hours, and not one person has come in to shop."

"You're kidding. I didn't know you were looking for work," Barb said as she opened the Crock-Pot to check on dinner.

Judy shrugged. "I wasn't looking for work. I was just feeling a little bored at home and wanted something to do that would allow me to socialize more, but to be honest, there's more socialization at home. I at least have the neighbors and Bob there. Though he's been off on these fishing trips lately."

Barb nodded. "Well, that's a shame they're not bringing in more customers. Why do you think that is?"

Judy shook her head as she looked around at all the jewelry on display. "You know, I can't figure it out. The jewelry here has a very beachy style to it, and it's absolutely stunning. Heck, I've already seen a couple pieces I'd like to get for myself, eventually. So it's not the inventory."

"Maybe it's the location?" Barb asked.

Judy glanced out of the window. "You may be right. I don't know if people know this store is here. I didn't even know it was here until I stopped at the pizza place next door. They were not finished making my pie, so I walked on over here to browse. The owner mentioned needing part-time help, and I thought it would be fun, but I'm bored out of my mind."

"Can you keep busy with little tasks around the store?" Barb asked.

"That's all done. I had a list, and I accomplished it in the first forty-five minutes of my time here. I'm starting to feel like this wasn't a good decision on my part. It's making me feel lonely. I was really thinking that I'd be working in a bustling store, like the ones you see at Washington Mall, where there's always someone to ring up or answer a question for. I pictured having coworkers I could chat with in a lively, fun atmosphere. There isn't any need for more than one person working at a time here in this small store. You know, it's nice to have the little extra money, but really, I don't need it. We're set with retirement."

Barb crossed her arms. "Was the store lively and fun when you first visited it?"

Judy paused for a moment. "Now that I think about it, it wasn't, but I figured it was because it was towards the end of the day. I had gotten there about thirty minutes before closing."

"Well, when do you work? I can come stop in and visit you," Barb said.

"Just two to three days a week. Not a whole lot. The owner is a young woman who just had a baby. I think she's trying to juggle this business and her first time at motherhood all at once."

Barb sighed. "I'm sure she can find someone else for a couple days a week. Why don't you head over to Washington Mall and find something more suitable for you?"

Judy nodded as she held up a sterling silver necklace with a large turquoise stone at the end. "I've thought about it, but I feel bad leaving so soon without giving it a real shot. Plus, I'm not *that* interested in finding a job. This just came up at the right time."

"What did you say the store name was?" Barb asked.

"Coastal Jewels," Judy said as she went back behind the counter and took a seat.

Just then, the door to the store opened, and Judy popped

out of her chair. "Barb! What are you doing here?" she asked as she looked at her phone.

Barb laughed as she hung up. "I decided to put you on speaker as I headed over to surprise you. I have to say, I see why this place isn't getting much business. The sign out front is tiny and covered by a huge bush. I only knew where it was because you mentioned the pizza shop next door."

"You're right. I should bring that up to the owner. I don't know how she's affording to keep this place open with barely any sales. It's truly a shame. She needs to do something," Judy said as she showed Barb around the store.

"Wow. It really is beautiful in here. From the beautiful jewelry to the beachy decorations … and what is that smell?"

Judy pointed to the counter. "We have a sea spray candle burning. Lovely, isn't it?"

"It's a nice touch. Does she make this jewelry?" Barb asked, holding up a beaded necklace.

"Some of it, but she also outsources pieces from local jewelry makers and even some not-so-local. She's got these gorgeous dried flower rings from a maker in Colorado. She really knows how to find great pieces," Judy said as she pointed to the rings by the window.

Barb followed Judy back to the counter. "I was thinking. Maybe this is a side venture for her. Perhaps she already has a job that brings in the money. Or maybe her husband does? This could possibly be her passion project? Maybe she's OK with business trickling in for the time being."

Judy shrugged. "I don't know, but this rent can't be cheap. That's a lot of money being spent on a passion project. Well, it's six o'clock. Time for me to close up the shop. Since you're here, feel like heading over to Schooners for a drink by the water?"

Barb smiled. "I was just going to ask you that exact question."

CHAPTER FOUR

Lisa sipped her hot coffee then took a bite of her cheese omelet at Uncle Bill's Pancake House. "It's gorgeous out. Finally, we have a day where it's not too humid and we can sit outside for breakfast."

Nick smiled and set his coffee cup down then glanced towards the beach. "It is. Should we go surfing before I head to the oyster farm?"

Lisa playfully rolled her eyes. "We certainly don't have enough time for that. Plus, I still have this rash from the last time we surfed," she said, holding up her arm.

"Jeez. That still hasn't gone down?" Nick asked as he reached out to touch Lisa's arm while inspecting it.

Lisa felt her skin start to sting. "No. If it doesn't get better in a few days, I'm going to have to make a doctor's appointment."

Nick shook his head as he took a bite of his blueberry pancakes. "Do you think it was from the board or something like a jellyfish?"

Lisa shrugged. "Beats me. I've been surfing for a long time, and this is a first. Maybe some sand got between me and the board."

"You should have worn your wet suit like I suggested. This would have all been avoided," Nick said with a smirk as he took another bite.

"You're right, I should have," Lisa said with a smile as she observed Nick meticulously pour syrup on his pancakes.

Lisa looked out towards the ocean, watching a couple riding bikes together on the street. She picked up her coffee, took a sip, and then caught Nick looking at her from the corner of her eye. "What? Do I have something on my face?"

Nick continued to stare. "No … I was just looking at you. You look extra beautiful today."

Lisa felt her face flush. "Why, thank you. So do you."

Nick dramatically flipped his hair with his hand. "You think?"

Lisa laughed just as the server came by and refilled their coffees. After the server left, Lisa turned serious. "I've been thinking … you've been spending all of this time at my place, but I haven't seen your house yet."

Nick cleared his throat then stared at his pancakes as he jabbed a fork into them. "I promise I'll have you over soon. The construction on the house has been taking a lot longer than they said. There are too many nails and boards lying around. It's really not safe to bring you around there."

Lisa nodded. "What kind of construction did you say it was? I don't remember."

Nick fumbled on his words. "Well, I'm having the carpet ripped up and am redoing the wood floors underneath it. The company keeps delaying the finish of it due to scheduling conflicts. I hope you don't mind that I've been staying over at your place lately."

"It's totally fine. I enjoy the company," Lisa said as she looked at Nick, trying to figure him out. "Maybe we can drive by your place. I'd like to at least see where it is. We've been dating for a bit now, and I still don't know where you live—"

Nick cut in. "I've been meaning to tell you I received tickets to an Eagles preseason game later this month."

Lisa felt her heart sink. As much as she'd love to go to an Eagles game, she could tell Nick was avoiding the subject of her seeing his house. The secrecy was starting to remind her of her ex-husband, who had established an entire other family while they were married. The red flags were there all over again. "That's great, I guess ..." Lisa said as she piled her dirty dishes up and pushed them to the end of the table.

Nick cocked his head to the side. "Are you alright?"

Lisa stood up from the table. "My stomach is suddenly not feeling well. I think we should ask for the check and head out. Unless, of course, you're not finished."

Nick looked at the last pancake left on his plate. "Nah, I'm good. I don't need the extra calories anyway," he said, standing up and waving to the server.

They paid, said their goodbyes, and went their separate ways in their cars.

Lisa started driving towards her house and called Donna on speaker phone.

"Hey, girl! I was just thinking of you. I just saw a VW van like the one you have roaming around Cape May," Donna said.

"Really? Well, that's cool," Lisa said. "Look, are you alone?"

Donna nodded. "I am. Just out walking on the Wildwood Boardwalk after checking in on our store. What's up?"

"Something fishy is going on with Nick, and I can't put my finger on it," Lisa said as she approached a stop sign.

"Like what?" Donna asked, her attention now fully focused on the conversation.

"We've been dating a couple months now, and we're always at my place. I have never seen where he lives. Whenever I bring up seeing his house, he has some excuse about why I can't go over there. Then, today, I asked about him and me possibly driving by so I could see *where* he lives, and he

28

completely changed the subject. It's just not adding up," Lisa said as she turned onto Sunset Boulevard.

"Huh. That is weird," Donna said as she stopped walking.

"Right? I don't want to go through this secrecy stuff again in another relationship. If I straight up confront him, will I possibly chase away a good thing? I really like him, like a lot. I want us to work, but this has really been bothering me."

"Didn't you already confront him by discussing why he doesn't want to bring you over there?" Donna asked as she started walking again.

Lisa shook her head. "No. That was me just asking again about his house. I've never brought up that it bothers me."

"Maybe you should tell him ..." Donna said as some seagulls swooped in on a fallen french fry in front of her on the boardwalk. "Or maybe—"

"What?" Lisa asked.

"I don't know. I was just thinking. Do you have his address?" Donna asked.

Lisa laughed. "That's the other thing. No, I don't know it. He's never told me. All I know is that he lives somewhere over by Pennsylvania Avenue."

"How do you know that?" Donna stopped walking again.

"We were on the phone while he was out for a night walk, and he mentioned that street," Lisa said as she pulled into her driveway.

Donna nodded. "Well, I have an idea. We're going to do a little investigating. Get out your dark sunglasses and headscarf. We're going undercover."

Lisa laughed. "Donna, come on. Be serious."

"I am being serious. I've been known in some circles as Sherlock Donna. I'm really good at finding information on the internet, and we're going to find his address, and then we're going to drive by to see his place."

Lisa bit her lip. "He'll see my car."

Donna rolled her eyes. "We're going to use my car, of

course, since he doesn't really know it. You'll be disguised and so will I. We'll get to the bottom of this."

Lisa felt her stomach turn. "I don't know. I'm suddenly nervous about what we will find."

Donna laughed. "What we will find? We're driving by a house in a neighborhood, not going to a murder scene."

"You know what I mean. This could make or break our new relationship."

Donna shrugged. "Well, do you want to do it or not?"

Lisa sighed. "I guess we can. Just don't tell anybody, and I mean *anybody*."

* * *

"I can't believe Sarah and Chris are all moved out," Margaret said as Dave pulled his truck into the bay house's driveway. "I feel sad about it. They won't be our neighbors anymore."

Dave nodded as he put the truck in park, then glanced towards Chris and Sarah's now vacant house. "It is sad, but we're never here, anyway. So it won't feel much different."

"I hear the new owners should be moving in tomorrow," Margaret said as she got out of the truck and slammed the door shut. "It will be interesting to see what they're like. Did they tell you anything about them?"

Dave shook his head as he got out of the truck and headed towards the front door of their house. "Nothing. I'm not sure if they know too much. I do know they got a nice penny for it, which has probably raised the value of our place."

Dave put the key in the front door's dead bolt but stopped and looked at Margaret. "Now, I want to say that I cleaned for a few hours on Saturday. This is what it looks like after."

"I'm sure it looks fine," Margaret said as Dave unlocked the door and they both stepped inside.

Dave shrugged as he looked at Margaret's shocked face.

"What happened in here? Did a bomb go off? You didn't

mention the scratches and marks all over the walls … or this torn wallpaper," Margaret said, walking around the living room, inspecting everything.

"I must have missed all of that when I was busy looking at the mountains of beer cans everywhere. Thankfully, that's at least gone now," Dave said as he walked towards the dining room.

"My vase!" Margaret yelled out. "They broke my beloved vase from my grandmother. I knew I should never have brought it here," Margaret said as she held up a large broken-off piece with tears in her eyes.

Dave walked over to her and put his hand on her shoulder. "I can fix that. You'll barely see the crack lines."

Margaret set the broken vase piece down and took a deep breath. "It was my fault for keeping a precious item like that in our rental. I should have known better. You don't have to fix it."

Dave felt his heart sink for his beloved wife. "I'm feeling pretty angry right now at how awful and inconsiderate people can be with other's properties. Angry that we have to take extra time out of our lives to clean up *their* mess. Yes, we can rightfully keep their security deposit, but it doesn't cover anywhere near the damage done."

Margaret rubbed Dave's arm. "Let's move forward. We'll clean this up today, and then we will have a long talk later about what changes we'll make in renting this house going forward."

Dave nodded and walked into the kitchen. "That sounds like a plan. I'm going to wipe out the fridge then sweep and mop in here."

Margaret opened a closet and pulled out some rags and all-purpose cleaner spray. "And I'll get the marks off the wall then vacuum the rugs and try to re-glue the wallpaper. Hopefully, we can get it all done before dinner."

* * *

By 5 p.m., they were driving back to their farmhouse with the windows down, feeling filthy and exhausted.

"Should we stop and pick up the girls?" Dave asked.

Margaret shook her head. "No, they're at my parents'. My mom cooked them dinner. They're going to drop them off at home around seven."

"Perfect. Well, what did you want to do for dinner?" Dave asked, feeling his stomach growl.

"I don't know, but I'm starving. Why don't we shower and get takeout? We're too tired to cook," Margaret said as they pulled onto their street.

"I agree with everything you just said," Dave said with a smile.

"I know we are dying to get inside and cleaned off, but can you stop by the Beach House Market before you pull into the driveway? This is the longest I've gone without checking it."

Dave cocked his head to the side. "You didn't check it this morning?"

"I didn't. I rushed out of the house to get to my doctor's appointment and run errands. It completely slipped my mind," Margaret said as they pulled up to the front of the market. They both got out of the truck and walked inside, and their eyes widened in disbelief.

"There is *so much* missing. The jalapeños are gone. The tomatoes are nearly gone. All of the flowers are gone," Margaret said as she walked around inspecting everything.

Dave walked towards the back counter. "You've only got a couple of zucchinis and yellow summer squash left. The potted herbs appear to have been taken too."

Margaret paused in thought. "What if someone just grabbed it all and took off? You hear about that happening at other honor system road stands from time to time. I've never had this much stuff missing before. I wish I was here to

32

restock in case other people were looking for flowers and produce."

Dave put the key into the lock on the money box and peered inside. "There's a ton of cash and checks in here. It's practically overflowing."

"Really?" Margaret asked excitedly.

"Yes," Dave said, pulling the loose bills and checks out and putting it on the counter. "We can count it all out to make sure nobody shorted us, though if they did, I'm not sure how we can do anything about it at this point."

Margaret shrugged. "We can count it out during dinner, but it's looking to me like we made out pretty well with our little farm market. I'm too excited to go in and shower. I want to go pick more from the gardens, so we're restocked for tomorrow."

Dave reached into his pocket and grabbed his cell phone. "How about this. I'll have a pizza delivered to the market. We'll restock together and eat dinner out here under the string lights with the fireflies."

"Now that sounds like the perfect date night," Margaret said, laughing as she reached under a bench and grabbed two baskets, handing one to Dave.

They walked to the gardens together, holding their baskets as Dave called in a pizza delivery. The cicadas grew louder and louder as the sky grew darker and darker.

Margaret picked a basket full of yellow Lemon Boy tomatoes then glanced over at Dave, who had finished picking a basket of pickling cucumbers. "Did you feel that?"

Dave stopped and looked at Margaret. "Feel what?"

Margaret felt another raindrop fall on her arm. "Rain."

Dave shook his head. "I thought that was just my sweat," he said with a chuckle.

"Are we supposed to get rain tonight?" Margaret asked as she looked up at the dark sky.

"Not that I've heard of … though this sky is a little too dark for 6 p.m. in the summer. These might be rain clouds," Dave said, looking up.

Just then, thunder boomed in the distance, and Margaret noticed the pizza delivery car pulling up in front of the market. "Dinner's here."

"So's the rain," Dave said as the raindrops started coming down harder. "Let's make a run for it to the market," he said as they both took off with their baskets.

Margaret laughed as she tried to balance the heavy tomatoes in her arms as she ran, noticing Dave was doing the same, which made her laugh harder. "I can't do this. I can't run while I'm laughing," Margaret said as she slowed into a walk.

Dave kept going, determined to get the pizza before the rain came down even harder.

By the time Margaret got to the market, the rain had started coming down in sheets, and she was soaked.

Dave smiled as he flicked on the white string lights around the market and propped open the pizza box. "Guess we got our showers out of the way," he said with a chuckle.

Margaret smiled as she picked up a hot slice and took a bite. "It doesn't get much better than this."

CHAPTER FIVE

"Oh, this is nice," Susan, one of the ladies on the women's retreat, said as they walked past tall sunflowers and into Willow Creek Winery and Farm.

Dolly smiled at the host then looked back at the group. "We've got a lot of people. Why don't we pair off in groups of three and four and sit at the patio tables?"

The host smiled as she picked up some menus. "Perfect. Follow me this way," she said, walking out the front door towards the tables.

Tonya—the fun-loving, never-married, childless one of the group—scanned the ladies as they walked outside. "You, you, and you, come sit with me at my table," she said, pointing at Kristen, Maggie, and Chrissy.

Kristen pointed to herself, feeling surprised. "Me?"

Tonya rolled her eyes. "Yes, *you*. Now, get over here," she said playfully as she took a seat at a shady table on the patio under an umbrella.

Kristen didn't know whether to feel honored or scared. She chose the former as she sat down with the rest of the elected group.

Tonya looked at her menu, dragging her finger down it as

she read then stopped on something. "Well, I hear the sangria is good here, so I'm getting the peach sangria."

The rest of the group nodded in agreement. "That sounds good to me," Maggie said.

"Perfect, maybe we can get a pitcher then," Tonya said as she took off her big cat-eye sunglasses and adjusted her multiple beaded necklaces around her neck while the bangles on her wrist clinked together per usual.

"Anyone hungry?" Chrissy asked.

"Sure am. How about the hummus platter and bruschetta for the table?" Kristen asked as she looked at the menu.

Tonya nodded, feeling proud of herself. "See, this is why I knew to pick you all for my table. We'd all agree on sharing everything. It's more fun when you share, don't you think?"

Maggie crossed her arms and made a face. "I guess, but don't ask me to share dessert."

Everyone at the table laughed loudly, while the rest of the ladies sitting together at the other tables looked over to see what the commotion was.

The drinks came, and the sangria was poured and gulped down. By the time the appetizers came, they were ready to devour them.

Tonya leaned back in her seat as she took another sip of her sangria. "Are you all liking your time in Cape May so far?"

"Yes, I'm loving the meshing of the farms, the old Victorians, and the beach life. You get a little bit of everything here," Kristen said as she took a bite of pita with hummus on it.

"Agreed," Maggie said as she looked toward the gorgeous vineyard before them. "It was neat to drive in here and see the chickens. I love how far back off the road on this quiet piece of land this winery is. We even passed a property with some horses grazing on the way here. Not too long ago, we were sitting on the beach listening to the ocean. It's the best of both worlds."

Chrissy nodded. "Everything they just said. They took the words right out of my mouth."

"So, Tonya … never married, you said?" Chrissy asked.

Tonya shook her head confidently. "Nope. Never. No kids either. I've had a couple long-term relationships, but I'm finally at a place where I'm happiest being alone. I can do what I want when I want without checking in with anyone. I don't have to worry about anyone but myself, and honestly, I've never felt more independent than in my seventies. I'm heading to Bar Harbor, Maine after I leave here. It's been one heck of an adventure these days."

Maggie held her hand up for a high five. "I'm loving that for you. I discovered, after forty years of marriage, that what was making me unhappy for years was indeed my marriage. I had been going to therapy, talking with friends, and I even changed my career to figure out what was bringing me down in life. I just couldn't put my finger on it. Then, during one of my therapy sessions, my therapist recommended going out and having a 'treat myself' day, so I did. I went and got a pedicure, then took myself to the city for a fancy brunch—alone. After-wards, I decided to go to an art museum, where I spent two hours marveling and learning about all of the pieces on display. There was still time in the day left, so I headed to the mall and tried on dresses for the first time in years. I splurged on two gorgeous dresses. I was feeling amazing and on top of the world. I get home with this high on life, and my husband is downright miserable. Instead of asking me about my day, he points at the clock and says he's starving. He berates me for not being back in time for dinner, which I normally took care of in our household. He says I should have texted. I explain that I lost track of time, which in all honesty, I did. I didn't think I'd be shopping and trying on dresses for an hour and a half—"

Kristen narrowed her eyes. "Who cares if you lost track of time? He should be able to make himself something to eat. He's an adult!"

Tonya and Chrissy nodded in agreement.

"You're absolutely right. We had a whole bunch of frozen meals in the freezer for days when there wasn't time to make anything. He could have easily popped one in the microwave or had a snack from the cupboard. What really drove it home for me, though, was he knew I had been struggling with finding my happiness. He knew I was heading out for a rare day to treat myself. He didn't care about any of that. He only cared about himself. Then, after I whipped him something up for dinner quickly, I sat on the porch alone with my thoughts. It was then that I thought about how, in our marriage, he always put himself first. My frustration lies in the fact that I'd never figured this out until many years later," Maggie said as she took a sip of her sangria. "Now, I'm sixty-two and trying to navigate this new life. I've never been happier, though."

Tonya punched the sky. "Yes! That last part. You've never been happier. Better late than never, no?"

Maggie smiled, feeling really good about where the conversation was going. "I feel like I've known you all for years. You're all so easy to talk to."

Kristen shrugged as she took a bite of the bruschetta. "The stories I could tell. I could gab all night! My loser ex-husband is off with his cupcake princess—you know, the one that worked at my store that he had an affair with. Did I mention she's twenty-six, and he's sixty-six? It's not going to last, and I'll have the last laugh. The fact is, him leaving me for her was the best thing to happen to me."

Tonya topped Kristen's sangria glass off with the last of the pitcher. "Man. I'd say I'm sorry, but it sounds like there's nothing to be sorry about. However, can we organize a group trip to throw cupcakes at his car?"

Kristen burst out laughing with everyone else at the table. Meanwhile, the rest of the ladies had finished up their drinks and crowded around their table.

"We want in on this funny conversation," Susan said.

Dolly butted in. "Ladies, how about a little early-evening swimming at Liz's house? It's surely hot enough for it. We can stop back at the Seahorse to change into bathing suits and grab towels and whatnot."

The ladies all glanced at each other, giddy as little kids. It was starting to feel like adult summer camp.

* * *

Margaret parked behind Oyster Bay Restaurant and walked through the back into the bar entrance, immediately spotting Dave sitting at the bar.

Dave smiled and patted the stool next to him. "Saved you a seat."

Margaret sat next to him and gave him a kiss on the cheek. "Why thank you. Gosh, it's crowded in here," she said while looking around the room.

"It is," Dave said as he eyed a bunch of people walking in the door. "It's the happening place to be, I guess."

Margaret glanced at the menu then set it down. "I'm getting my usual. The Cape Cobb salad and a glass of pinot grigio."

Dave set his menu down too. "I think I'm doing the usual, as well. Beer and a burger. By the way, where are the girls? I thought they were coming tonight."

Margaret laughed. "They're having dinner with Liz, Greg, and the boys then swimming afterwards in their pool. I thought it'd be good if it was just the two of us tonight, so we can discuss the bay house."

Before Dave could respond, the bartender was in front of them, taking their drink and food orders. Moments after that, they both had their drinks.

"Where were we?" Dave asked as he took a sip of his beer and turned his stool slightly towards Margaret so their legs were touching.

"The bay house," Margaret said as she swished her white wine in the glass. "Particularly the future of it. Should we have stricter rules? Should we vet people better?"

Dave thought for a moment. "I was thinking that might be something that could prevent the issues we've had this summer. Then again, isn't it common decency to not destroy someone's house and leave trash everywhere? Do people need a rule stating not to do that these days? And even then, is a written rule really going to stop them?"

Margaret sipped her wine, then nodded. "You're right. If losing their security deposit isn't deterring them, what will? Maybe vetting renters more thoroughly will work better?"

Dave shook his head. "I'm not sure how we can do that. We ask all the right questions before approving bookings. The last renters obviously lied about the number of people staying there. According to Chris and Sarah, it was like a big ol' party at the house with lots of people."

Their food arrived, and Margaret poured her green goddess dressing onto her salad then took a bite and swallowed. "How much of a profit have we made off the rental so far this summer?"

Dave took a bite of his burger, swallowed, then wiped his mouth with his napkin. "That's another thing I wanted to bring up. After all the expenses on our end, it's a few thousand. By the end of the summer, it might be about double that if there aren't any more cancellations or destruction."

Margaret rubbed her chin. "So around six thousand. That's not bad."

Dave shrugged. "It isn't, but we haven't factored in all the time we've spent cleaning and doing laundry between renters, mowing the property, and fixing things that break between renters. Is this something we want to continuously put our time into?"

Margaret took a sip of her wine. "We could have a realtor take over the listing instead of doing it ourselves? That would take a big load off us. We could also increase the price to deter the destructive renters from renting, and we could have stricter cancellation policies."

Dave sat back in his stool and crossed his arms, noticing the entire bar and tables surrounding it was packed with patrons and the noise level was getting louder. "I have a better idea. Why don't we put the bay house up for sale?"

Margaret dropped her fork on her plate. "You can't be serious. Why would you want to give up that wonderful house?"

Dave looked around the room in thought, his eyes landing on a family with a husband and wife and two young daughters sharing an appetizer. "It's a great house in a great spot, but we're never there. It's mostly an investment property at this point. Chris and Sarah's house just sold for double what Chris bought it for. I'm pretty sure we could get around the same price. I was thinking we could use the money for renovations on the farmhouse or maybe—"

Margaret cut in. "Buy a different investment property."

Dave smiled. "That was my other idea. I've been itching for a new project since completing the Beach House Market. Building it got my juices flowing, and I want to take on something bigger. I was thinking I could build a deck behind the farmhouse, but I already know I could finish that pretty quickly, especially with some help. I want a long-term project. We've already found our dream home and property. Maybe I could renovate a cheap old run-down property from top to bottom. Maybe even flip it if need be or rent it out, but with a realtor this time."

Margaret felt herself growing excited. "I think you're onto something."

"So you're on board with selling it?" Dave asked.

Margaret nodded. "I think now is an ideal time to sell, and it sounds like we're ready for that. You're right, we're never there except to clean, and with Chris and Sarah moving out to a nicer place, it feels a little lonely over there."

Dave's eyes glazed over in thought. "Maybe we can find something closer to the ocean. That would be a dream."

Margaret chuckled. "Those Cape May houses by the beach go for a million or more. I don't know if that's in our budget."

Dave nodded. "You're right, but maybe I can get to something that's run-down before anyone else. Just think of how nice it would be to have a place to walk back to after a day on the beach where the family can shower and eat, then listen to the waves crashing in the distance."

Margaret smiled as she took a sip of her wine. "Sounds familiar. You do know I'm part owner of the Seahorse Inn, right?"

Dave laughed. "I know, but a single-family house is different than the inn. We could rent it out with realtors, and we could charge so much more than the bay house since it's closer to the beach. Plus, it's there for when family and friends want to use it without having strangers staying in the other rooms next to them, like the inn. It would be quaint and cozy."

"It does sound dreamy, but I think it's going to be hard. Investors are probably foaming at the mouth to find a property like the one you'd be looking for. They could probably outbid you easily too. Maybe something in West Cape May might be more attainable, no?"

Dave cracked his knuckles. "Maybe, but I have some big dreams, and where there's a will, there's a way."

CHAPTER SIX

Dave and Margaret pulled up to the Cape May Harbor full of docked boats and walked towards Chris and Sarah's new house right on the water.

Margaret looked out at the sunlight sparkling on the water. "Wow, I see the appeal of moving here. It's so serene and gorgeous."

They approached a tall, modern home with gray siding and entered through the back door. "Hello? Anyone home?" Margaret called out.

Sarah approached the door, decked out in a button-down white shirt, blue jeans, and loafers. "Hey, guys! Welcome to our new place. Come in," Sarah said as she gave both Margaret and Dave a hug.

Margaret pointed at Sarah. "I see you're embracing the boat/harbor life pretty quickly," she said with a chuckle.

Sarah waved her hand in the air. "I just threw this on. Wasn't even thinking anything of it. Anyway, come with me up the steps to the kitchen, where everyone is hanging out."

They followed Sarah to the third floor, where there was a chef's kitchen and huge living room with a sectional sofa and tall windows that faced out towards the harbor, letting in sunlight at every angle. Their friends and Liz and Greg were also there.

Liz took a sip of her red wine and waved at Margaret and Dave. "Once you stop gawking, come over here and try my cheese board."

Donna laughed. "Yes, please try the charcuterie. Liz hasn't stopped talking about it."

Liz playfully rolled her eyes. "I'm sorry if I'm proud of my creation. I spent a lot of time working on it."

Greg nodded as he spread some brie on a cracker, drizzled honey on it, then took a bite and swallowed. "She did. She had to have the best olives, the crunchiest grapes, imported salami, and hand-picked cheeses that she sampled at the counter. It was a … process, but we made it out alive."

Liz popped a grape into her mouth. "We were only there for a half hour."

Greg raised his eyebrow and chuckled. "Try an hour. You had that cheese counter guy working for his check. I'll say that."

Margaret ate a piece of salami and then looked around the room. "This place looks brand-new. Was it just built last year?"

Chris walked over from his conversation with Dale, holding a beer. "It's about ten years old. You guys ready for the full tour? We were waiting for you and Dave to get here first."

Everyone nodded as Chris walked towards the windows. He then opened the sliding glass door onto the third-floor porch. "We'll start with Sarah's favorite thing about the house first."

The group stepped out onto the large deck with gorgeous waterfront views of the harbor and wetlands. Out there was a long table with chairs, a gas grill, and a sitting area with cushioned chairs and ottomans.

"This is really luxurious," Liz said as she sat down in a chair and kicked her feet up on the ottoman. "It feels like a vacation rental."

Chris pointed to the right. "Look, here comes a blue heron flying past."

Everyone gawked as the heron glided by right in front of them.

"It's like a front-row seat to nature out here," Donna said as she grabbed Dale's hand.

"It really is. I feel so lucky that we got this place," Sarah said as she eyed some boats pulling into the harbor.

Chris pointed below. "I finally have a house with its own boat slip too."

"Are you bringing one of the birding boats over here?" Greg asked.

Chris shook his head. "No, they'll stay over at the dock they've been at, but I did get a new boat recently. It's in the slip now."

Dave peered down at the boat slip. "That huge boat there?"

Chris looked down at the boat. "Yep, that's it. A beauty, isn't it?"

Dave widened his eyes. "It looks really expensive."

Chris nodded. "It is. I've got my work cut out for me with it. It does need a bit of fixing up."

Sarah walked back into the house. "Let's tour the rest of our new place. Wait until you see the sitting room on the second floor."

The group followed Sarah and Chris through the third floor and down to the second floor. Meanwhile, Liz nudged Margaret in the back. "How did they afford this? This place is not anywhere in the same ballpark as the place they sold," she whispered.

Margaret shrugged. "I don't know. I feel like I'm in a rich person's home, though. It's super fancy here."

Sarah opened a door and pointed inside. "Here's our bedroom. As you can see, we have amazing views out onto the harbor and another deck right off the room. Plus the en suite bath, of course."

"This is really nice. A huge upgrade from the bay house you just sold, no?" Donna asked as she peered out the windows.

"It is. We feel really lucky," Chris said as he put his arm around Sarah.

Sarah smiled as they led everyone to the other bedrooms, the extra sitting room, then down onto the first floor and to the outdoor patio facing the water.

Everyone stood around on the patio, looking at all the docked boats and listening to the sounds of the shorebirds around them.

"So, I know what you're all thinking," Chris said as he took a sip of his beer. "How did we afford this place."

Greg cleared his throat. "Well, duh."

Everyone laughed while Liz nudged Greg.

"I received a surprise inheritance from my uncle that passed a few months ago. This was his second home, and that's his boat. He left it all to me. I wasn't expecting it, honestly. He never married or had kids, and besides my parents, I was the closest relative to him. He left my parents a bunch of money and me all of this," Chris said as he looked toward the boat and back at everyone. "It was the surprise of a lifetime. I didn't want to tell anyone initially, but now I feel better speaking more freely about it, at least to close friends and family. I've always worked for everything I've had, and to have something like this handed to me felt really foreign and wrong at first. I had a hard time with it, if you can believe that."

Sarah nodded. "He did. He didn't want the house or boat initially. We had to have a family discussion with his parents about it, and then we had to discuss what our plan was with the bay house."

Margaret looked at Liz then at Chris and Sarah. "We had something similar happen with the Seahorse Inn. Our great-aunt left it to us. She's still around doing her thing, but she didn't want it anymore."

"That's right," Sarah said as she smiled up at Chris. "See, you're not alone."

Chris smiled, then glanced at Margaret and Dave. "Do you two miss us over at the bay house yet?"

Dave chuckled. "Of course. It's not the same without you two living next door … even if Margaret and I are never there."

Margaret smirked at Dave. "Should we tell everyone?"

"What?" Liz asked.

Dave cleared his throat. "We're selling the bay house."

Sarah dropped her mouth open. "What? Why?"

"After a lackluster rental summer, we've decided we'd like to sell it and pursue other things," Dave said as he took a sip of his beer.

Margaret smiled. "Dave wants a project, so we're hoping to find a cheap property in Cape May, possibly on the outskirts, to renovate and build on. It would most likely be another investment property, since we are very happy at the farmhouse."

Dave nodded. "The farmhouse is our dream home. I don't think we'll ever leave there, but yeah, I've got the bug to build like never before. I can't tell you how being here at your new place has made me even more excited about it."

"That's really great, man," Chris said, giving Dave a pat on the back. "I wish you luck."

"Well, if you need any furniture in the new place, I'm your lady," Liz said, pointing to herself.

"How's the furniture restoration business going?" Sarah asked.

Liz glanced at Greg and smiled. "It's going alright. I'm outgrowing my garage workshop. I've been finding a lot more furniture to restore lately, and I'm running out of storage room in the garage. Also, the boys have taken an interest in helping me, so I've been finishing pieces a lot quicker. It's a good problem to have, I guess."

Greg put his arm around Liz. "I told her she should look for a retail space somewhere in Cape May to sell her restored furniture. Maybe then I can get my garage back," he said with a chuckle.

Liz shrugged. "I'd really like to avoid the overhead of renting a retail space, not to mention hiring employees. Working at home gives me a sense of freedom. There aren't set hours. I don't have to worry about getting up early to open a shop or staying all day to close it up."

"I get that. I love owning the Book Nook, but I'm so glad I have employees that I can depend on to keep the store running without me there," Sarah said just as Lisa came walking up from the driveway.

"Hey, guys. Sorry I'm so late. I had to handle some buyer payment issues over the phone. I didn't expect it to take over an hour of my time," Lisa said as she dropped her purse onto a chair.

"You didn't miss much. Just the tour of the new house and some amazing charcuterie," Chris said.

"Don't worry, I'll give you the tour plus all of the cheese you want when we go back inside," Sarah said as she gave Lisa a hug.

"Where's Nick?" Donna asked as everyone headed back inside.

"He's over at the oyster farm. I guess it's low tide, so they had to get some stuff done over there."

"Is he still being secretive about his house?" Donna whispered.

Lisa nodded. "Yes. It's bothering me even more lately."

"Well, I have a plan for tomorrow," Donna said. "I'll pick you up around one."

* * *

Back at Coastal Jewels, Judy stood at the counter of the empty jewelry store, doodling on a notepad. She watched some cars pass by outside the window, then sighed as she looked at the clock on the wall, noticing she still had two long hours left of her shift.

The door opened, and in walked Tammy, the owner, with her new baby in a stroller. "Hi there," she said happily as she parked the stroller by the counter. "How's it going? Any shoppers visit today?"

Judy shook her head. "It's been pretty slow. Not many," Judy said, not having the heart to tell her that *not many* meant *nobody*.

Tammy nodded and looked towards the jewelry beautifully displayed around the store. "It's been a pretty rough start with this store, that's for sure."

"Is this your only business venture at the moment?" Judy asked.

"Yes. I used to sell the jewelry I made on Etsy. It went so well that I decided to expand to a storefront, but at this rate, I don't know how long I'll be able to keep this store open. Nobody is coming in, let alone buying anything," Tammy said as tears started forming in her eyes. "This was a dream of mine for years, to open my store right here in Cape May. What's good about it is I'm selling jewelry from many designers in addition to my own. That frees up some time to be with my baby. Before, I was working twenty-hour days getting jewelry pieces made. It brought in the money, but it took over my life. I can't live that way now, nor do I want to," she said, glancing over at her baby peacefully sleeping in the stroller.

Judy pointed outside. "One thing I've noticed is nobody can see the sign to the store when driving past. Not only is it small, it's blocked out by the huge overgrown bush. Maybe you can start with that."

"My husband brought that up to me, but I didn't listen. You're right. I should have that sign fixed soon."

"I also think the huge overgrown evergreens in front of the store need to be trimmed back to show that an actual store is behind all of it," Judy said.

"I agree. It all needs to be tidied up, but what else? What can I do to actually get customers in the store?" Tammy asked as she walked around the store, racking her brain.

"You could run a sale, maybe have some snacks and drinks and post about it on social media. My daughter, Margaret, is really good with that kind of stuff. She helps raise money for the Pinetree Wildlife Refuge," Judy said as she started dusting some areas around the store.

Tammy groaned. "Social media. There it is. I've avoided being on it all these years, but I guess with this jewelry store, I'm going to have to bite the bullet and make a business account."

Judy stopped in her tracks. "Well, there you go. I think posting on social media will definitely help spread the word about your shop. In the meantime, you can get the landlord to trim the overgrowth out front and put in a better sign. It might take a little time to get the ball rolling, but I think those changes will definitely push it in the right direction."

Tammy walked over to Judy and hugged her tightly. "You've just filled me with optimism and hope that I haven't had for this jewelry store in months. I really need this place to do well, especially since my husband just got laid off."

Judy held her hand over her mouth. "Oh, no. I'm so sorry to hear that."

Tammy nodded solemnly. "It was completely unexpected. The big company he works for did a mass layoff. While he knew about the upcoming layoffs, he didn't know he'd be part of it. He was initially told he was keeping his job. So it's been an especially rough month in our household. He's frantically looking for other work, and I'm here with this business that I'm losing money on while trying to be a good first-time mother to our newborn," she said, looking at her phone. "How do I even make a social media account? Can I do it on my phone?"

Judy smiled. "I'll see if my daughter, Margaret, has a couple hours this week to spare to help you. She's really good with social media. Me, not so much. I just know the basics, and even then, I forget my password regularly."

Tammy laughed. "Thank you. I really appreciate your help."

CHAPTER SEVEN

Donna pulled her car into Lisa's driveway and honked the horn.

Moments later, Lisa waved as she approached, then got into the passenger side, laughing. "A headscarf and sunglasses? You weren't joking."

Donna smirked. "What can I say? This has brought out the detective in me. I got you a headscarf too," she said while reaching into her bag in the back seat.

Lisa shook her head. "I'm not wearing that."

Donna lowered her sunglasses. "If we're going to do this, we have to be undercover. It's the only way it will work."

Lisa put her hand out. "Fine. Give me the scarf."

Donna handed her the scarf, and Lisa tied it around her head then put on her dark sunglasses.

"We look like twins," Lisa said, laughing.

Donna reached back into her bag, pulling out two sets of binoculars. "Can't forget these," she said, placing them in Lisa's lap. "Hold on to them for when we need them."

Lisa ripped her sunglasses off. "Donna, binoculars are way too obvious. If the neighbors see, they will take down your license plate."

Donna waved her hand in the air. "They won't see anything," she said as she put the car in drive and headed off across town.

The windows were down, and their headscarves flapped in the breeze as Donna turned the radio up when "Danger Zone" came on.

Lisa laughed. "Really? This song? Right now?"

Donna shrugged. "It's the theme."

Lisa watched Donna turn out of Cape May Point and out towards Sunset Boulevard. "How do you know where to go?"

Donna glanced at Lisa. "I googled him. He lives on Missouri Avenue."

"How do you know that's his current address? That might not be accurate."

"It said it's the most current address. I just have a hunch it's right," Donna said while turning towards Lafayette Street.

"I'm having second thoughts. We probably shouldn't be doing this," Lisa said as anxiety creeped through her.

"Lisa, we're just driving down a public street in Cape May. We aren't doing anything wrong. He's at the oyster farm, right?" Donna asked as they approached Missouri Avenue.

Lisa nodded. "That's what he told me."

"Well, then, don't worry about it. It's not like he's home to see anything. Plus, even if it he was, he doesn't know my car," Donna said as she started slowly driving down Missouri.

"What's the house number?" Lisa asked as she looked at each house that they passed.

"I think this is it ... 1821 ... right here," Donna said as she almost came to a full stop in front of a cute green rancher.

Lisa looked at the house then back at Donna. "This can't be it. He said his house is under construction. Maybe he lived here previously, and his new address hasn't been updated online yet."

"It's possible," Donna said as she stared at the house, noticing, through the window, an older couple sitting in the living room. "Well, those people certainly don't appear to be Nick."

"Who?" Lisa asked as she strained her neck to see.

"See, there. I think one of them is opening the front door now," Donna said, pointing.

Lisa ducked down in her seat. "Probably seeing why we're staring at their house."

Donna watched as the older gentleman threw a handful of birdseed out onto the steps. "No, looks like he was just giving the birds a snack, but I think our detective work has come to an end for today. This house is obviously not Nick's."

"OK, let's get out of here then. I feel silly with this head-scarf on," Lisa said as she pulled it off along with the sunglasses. Donna did the same.

"Well, since we're over this way, let's head over to Lucky Bones for some food," Donna said as she put the car into drive but kept her foot on the brake.

Lisa pulled down the passenger-side mirror and fixed her hair. "Sounds good," she said as she took one last look in the mirror, noticing a familiar car driving up behind them. "It's him."

"Who?" Donna asked.

"It's Nick. I'm pretty sure that's his car coming up the road behind us," Lisa said as she slinked down into her seat.

"You said he was working. How could that be him? Maybe it's someone else that has the same car," Donna said as she stared in the rearview mirror. "Oh, wait ... the car is pulling into the driveway."

Lisa slid down even lower in her seat. "In the green house's driveway? The one we thought he lived in?"

"Yes," Donna said as she put her sunglasses back on.

"Is it him? I'm afraid to look."

Donna discreetly watched. "Well, they're getting out of the car now. I see two legs——"

Lisa grew impatient. "Well, is it him or not?"

Donna paused for a moment then turned to Lisa. "It's him."

Lisa felt a pit in her stomach as she practically sat on the floor of the car. "Did he see you?"

Donna shook her head. "He never even looked over here. I don't think so. He just walked right into the house and shut the door."

"Well, we need to get out of here now before he comes back outside and sees us peering into his house that I'm not even supposed to know about," Lisa said.

"I'm on it," Donna said as she put the car into drive and headed out of the neighborhood. "Are we still going to Lucky Bones, though?"

Lisa crawled back up into her seat. "I guess, but I don't know how I'm going to eat anything. My stomach is in knots, and I just discovered that I've been lied to once again by a man."

"There could be a reason for why he lied. We don't know anything really," Donna said, feeling bad for Lisa.

"Possibly, but even if there is a good reason, do I really want someone who lies so easily in my life? I dealt with this with my ex-husband, and I promised myself I'd never deal with it again, and here I am. I'm just so … angry right now. I'm upset."

Donna nodded. "I get it. How about I buy you a glass of wine and we can discuss this at the restaurant?"

Lisa clenched her jaw. "I'm thinking you need to drive back to his house."

"What? No, we're not going to do that. What are we going to tell him? That we searched online for his address? It's a bad look," Donna said.

"I don't care. Lying and being secretive is a bad look. He's purposely never told me where he lives, and he lied about it being under construction. It also looks like he lied about being at work today," Lisa said, feeling more frustrated by the minute.

"OK, we're *not* going back to his house. I should never have initiated this little detective adventure, either. I didn't realize it would open this big can of worms. What I think you need to do is have a sit-down talk with him. Be as honest as possible, and tell him he has to be completely honest for this relationship to work."

Lisa took a deep breath. "You're right. I shouldn't jump to conclusions until we talk one-on-one about everything that's been on my mind. It might chase him away, but that's the chance I'm willing to take. I just can't make the same mistake twice."

Donna nodded, feeling better about the situation already. "Good. Well, a glass of wine is still on me," she said pulling into the parking lot of the restaurant.

* * *

Margaret led the women's retreat group across her farmhouse property for the grand tour while fanning herself. "Is it ninety-five degrees today?" she asked as she looked back at the ladies.

Samantha dabbed the sweat on her forehead with a paper towel. "Something like that. The humidity must be sky-high too."

"This has got to be the hottest it's been since we arrived in Cape May," Maggie said as she pulled her hat down lower on her head.

Margaret nodded as she pointed ahead. "Once we get to the greenhouse and lighthouse back past the lake, it's much shadier."

Kristen sighed as she looked up at the sun then at the distance they still had to walk. "Well, thank goodness. I don't know how much more I can walk with this sun beating down."

Margaret didn't hear and kept trucking ahead, rolling up her short sleeves so she was now wearing a tank top.

Eight minutes later, they stood in front of the lighthouse, breathing heavily and holding their clothes away from their bodies to air themselves out.

"Here it is. Our very own miniature lighthouse," Margaret said as she held out her arms towards the structure.

Chrissy looked it up and down. "Does it work?"

"Oh no. It's just a replica. You can go inside if you'd like to look around," Margaret said, leading the way to the door.

A few of the ladies followed her, peeking inside.

"It's much too hot in here," Becky said as she stepped inside then quickly exited.

Margaret pointed to the left. "That's our little greenhouse that came with the property, and back there behind the trees is a small creek. That decking there was built by Dave. We host tea party gatherings there from time to time."

"That all sounds swell, but how about some seats in the shade? Got any of that?" Tonya asked as she looked around.

"Actually, I do. I can pull some chairs out for you if you'd like," Margaret said as she headed towards the shed.

Tonya waved her hand in the air as she sat down on the ground. "Never mind. This will do."

"I thought I'd show you the flower and vegetable gardens next. We can take a rest in the shade first, if you'd all like," Margaret said then took a sip of cold water from her bottle. "Everyone is good on water still?"

Maryanne held up her bottle. "So far, so good, but I'll probably run out soon."

Darlene nodded. "It's only going to get hotter over the next few hours. Why don't we head over to the gardens now."

"Alright, I'm up," Tonya said as she stood back up and dusted herself off. "Show us to the flowers."

Ten minutes later, they'd trucked across the property, this

time with a little more shade from the oaks, and had arrived at the sunflower and zinnia patch.

"Does anyone want to cut some flowers for a bouquet?" Margaret asked as she held up some pruners.

"Me," Tonya yelled as she walked over and grabbed a pair with Susan and Chrissy.

"Ladies, help me find some good ones to cut, would you?" Tonya said as she maneuvered her way through the large flower patch with the group following behind.

"Ow. What was that?" Kristen asked as she slapped her leg.

Darlene waved her hands in front of her face. "They're all over me. There are hundreds of them."

"Mosquitos?" Becky asked.

Margaret swatted a few bugs away as she walked towards the house to turn off the irrigation system. "It looks like it. We can head back to the house if you all want," she yelled back.

Tonya shook her head. "Let me just cut a bouquet first. I've always wanted to do this," she said as she slapped some more mosquitos off her legs and stepped farther into the garden. "Wait. What's this? Is it a zinnia?" she asked the ladies standing behind her.

"Let me see," Chrissy said as she stepped forward into some hole in the ground, causing her to fall. She grabbed Tonya's shirt, and Tonya grabbed Kristen, who grabbed Darlene and Susan, causing all of them to fall while screaming.

"Really?" Tonya said as she sat on the ground. She laughed while looking at all of them sitting in a pile of mud. "We're completely covered from head to toe."

Kristen laughed. "And we just crushed about twenty flowers on the way down."

"Margaret!" Darlene yelled. "Bring the hose on over here. We look like mud rats."

"At least the bugs have left us alone," Susan said, laughing.

Margaret walked back with the hose, covering her mouth with her hand. "What happened?"

Tonya stood up and shook her head. "Apparently, none of us have any coordination. Care to wash us off?"

"You got it," Margaret said while spraying them down on the grass. "I have towels inside for everyone. Liz has invited us all over for some swimming at her pool. Are you all interested?"

"Need you ask in this heat? Yes," Becky said as she plucked a zinnia and stuck it in her hair.

"Perfect. I'll get the towels, and we'll head over. Follow me back to the house," Margaret said.

Moments later, they were all walking down shady back roads to Liz's house.

"I didn't realize we'd be walking," Susan said as she stumbled along in flip-flops.

Darlene shrugged as she put her towel around her neck. "Margaret said it's only a quarter mile down the road. Should be a pretty quick walk, I'm guessing."

"I hope so," Susan whispered back. "I'm getting too old for this weather."

Twenty minutes later, they were all in Liz and Greg's pool, relaxing on floats.

"I've got some snacks and drinks for everyone," Liz said as she walked out with a tray containing chips, French onion dip, and some cut-up fruit. "Help yourself to the drinks in the cooler."

"Thank you, Liz. You're wonderful," Tonya said as she dipped her shoulders underwater.

Margaret was standing in the pool, leaning up against the side, when she noticed Judy walking across the yard. "Mom?"

Judy walked through the pool gate and waved to everyone. "Hi, I'm Liz and Margaret's mom. I thought I'd come by and meet this fabulous group of women I've been hearing about."

The group said hello and introduced themselves while Judy took a seat in a lounge chair.

"What are you up to today?" Margaret asked.

Judy sighed. "A lot. I need your help."

"Help? With what?"

Judy leaned forward. "Coastal Jewels, the jewelry shop I got a part-time job at … it's struggling to make any business. The owner, Tammy, has a new baby, and while I was brainstorming with her about ways to drum up business, she said she doesn't do social media. I think it could really help."

Margaret nodded. "I get it. Well, can she stop by Liz's with her laptop today? I can spend some time with her setting up a business account and showing her the ropes."

"I'll text her now," Judy said as she pulled out her phone and started typing. She paused and looked at Margaret and Liz. "You two should see the amazing jewelry she sells there."

"Did I hear something about jewelry?" Tonya asked from across the pool.

"You did. I'm working at a small jewelry store. It has some of the most gorgeous beachwear jewelry I've seen. Problem is, nobody shops there."

"Well, I'm sure all of us ladies here can schedule a visit there together, no?" Tonya asked, looking around at the group.

"Definitely. I'd loved to find a nice statement piece necklace," Kristen said as she floated by on an inflatable dolphin.

"I'm down," Darlene said as she got out of the pool to grab a drink.

The rest of the group responded affirmatively, and Judy couldn't have felt more grateful.

CHAPTER EIGHT

"I just wanted one last look around before we meet with the realtor. I don't know why I feel so sentimental about this place," Margaret said as she walked through the living room and out onto the screened-in front porch.

"I know what you mean," Dave said as he took a seat on the porch. "It's the perfect quiet street right across from the bay. We had some good times here in the short period we had it."

Margaret sat next to Dave in the other chair then looked across the street towards the bay beach. "I'm remembering when we went for a walk along the beach and there were so many horseshoe crabs washed up ashore. The girls delicately flipped them back over for an hour to save them. They didn't want to stop until they saved them all."

Dave chuckled. "How could I forget? How about the time we grilled out back and I accidentally burned all the hot dogs and burgers."

Margaret laughed. "Oh, I definitely remember that. Abby was in tears. For some reason, she was dead set on eating a hot dog for dinner."

"It's funny how it just so happened that Chris and Sarah were getting ready to grill hot dogs and burgers next door that day. We joined them, and it ended up being the best evening," Dave said as he looked off into the distance, smiling.

Margaret reached over and grabbed Dave's hand. "We don't have to sell this place if you don't want to."

"I know, but it's the right time to do it. Our friends moved out next door, and this house is now worth a lot more than what I bought it for," Dave said as he put his other hand on top of Margaret's.

Margaret nodded. "You're right. I think it's the best decision for us."

Dave smirked. "Plus, I've already started looking around for a fixer-upper."

"Not shocking." Margaret smiled.

Dave looked out towards the street, noticing a bright-red sedan had pulled up in front the house. "I think that's the realtor."

They both stood up and walked out of the front porch to greet her.

"Hi, guys!" the realtor blurted out. "I'm Melissa, and this is Ben, my photographer," she said, pointing. Ben waved quickly, then started cleaning his camera lens.

"Nice to meet you, Melissa. We spoke on the phone. I'm Dave, and this is my wife, Margaret," Dave said as both Margaret and he shook hands with Melissa.

"Great. Great. So, I guess we'll get started. Ben is a master at photographing houses for listings. He'll begin with that while we go over the house together. I want to get your listing up as soon as possible," Melissa said as she followed Dave up the steps and onto the front porch.

"How quaint and cute is this screened-in front porch? People search for this kind of porch. Perfect for watching the sunset across the street without the bugs. I'm loving it," Melissa said as she walked through the front door.

"Oh, I'm in love. This living room is adorable. From the built-in bookshelves to the original crown molding and hardwood floors. What a gem this place is," Melissa said as she headed down the hall towards the kitchen with Margaret and Dave following behind.

Meanwhile, Ben was opening all the blinds around the house and moving little things around to establish the perfect lighting in the dining room.

Margaret nudged Dave. "Thank you, Melissa. Dave put a lot of work into this place. It really is such a great little house."

Melissa stood in the kitchen. "There's so much gorgeous natural light in here, and the appliances are modern and sleek. Wonderful tiling too … You said it's three bedrooms, right?"

Dave nodded. "Yes, with a nice-sized backyard too."

Melissa nodded and took a seat at the kitchen table. "I'm going to be upfront and honest. This place is going to sell fast. I may not even get a chance to do an open house."

Dave pointed next door. "I believe it. Our friends next door sold pretty quickly."

Melissa looked out the window next to her. "They sure did … but I think this house will sell even faster. Why? This part of town is booming lately, and people love the quiet that comes with the bay, and you've got that coveted front porch."

Ben walked into the room, holding his camera. "I'm almost done. Just have to get the backyard," he said while walking out the back door.

Melissa looked back towards Margaret and Dave. "I'll have this listing with photos up by tonight. We're going to start by pricing high. If there aren't any bites, we'll lower it, but I have a feeling that won't be necessary."

"I'm done," Ben said as he came back inside, shutting the back door behind him. "These photos came out great. It's a great place you have here," he said as he eyed the kitchen.

"Thank you. It is a special little place," Dave said as he put his arm around Margaret's shoulders.

Melissa stood up from the table. "Well, that's about all I need. I'll be in touch once I get the listing up, and then we'll go from there. It might be an exciting ride, so hold on," she said while shaking hands with Margaret and Dave.

They all headed out of the house together as Melissa and Ben got back in the car and took off.

Dave turned to Margaret. "Want to go check on the Beach House Market? I have a feeling we need to restock, and there's a couple little things I want to fix that have been bugging me."

"Sounds like a plan," Margaret said as she walked to the truck and hopped into the driver's side. "I'll drive."

Twenty minutes later, Margaret pulled the truck up in front of the Beach House Market and put it in park. "I can't get over how cute you made the market. I mean, look at those shutters."

Dave chuckled as he got out of the truck and closed the door. He walked towards the market with Margaret behind him. As they got closer, they both stopped in their tracks.

"Why does it look so bare in there?" Margaret asked as she started walking closer. "There's no way all those zucchinis are gone already. We usually only sell ten a day."

Dave held up the empty basket then looked down at the floor. "There's your answer."

Margaret looked down and widened her eyes. "What is this? Why are there pieces of zucchini everywhere? Is this some sort of prank?"

Dave leaned down and picked up a half of a zucchini then showed it to Margaret. "Not a prank. Critters. See the bite marks?"

Margaret shook her head. "So some raccoons and squirrels and whatever else just came in here and had a feast, huh?"

Dave nodded. "I think they found their five-star restaurant."

Margaret tried not to laugh, but she couldn't help it. "How are we going to stop this from happening again?"

"Well, we're probably just going to have to close the doors

on the market in the evening. The daytime is too busy with customers and us for the critters to get very far. This definitely happened overnight," Dave said as he threw the chewed-up zucchini out onto the lawn. He then looked at his watch. "I have to get over to the refuge. I'm filling in for Herb. He had to get over to a doctor's appointment. We're trying to have these new vulture enclosures ready by tomorrow."

"You're a needed man," Margaret said as she smiled and squeezed his arm.

* * *

"Bob, just pull up in front of the store," Judy said as she clutched a stack of papers and hopped out of the passenger seat of the car. "I'll be right back."

Bob chuckled. "I know, dear. We've already done this about ten times today."

Minutes later, Judy got back in the car with half the stack of papers. "I think that about does it."

"We're done?" Bob asked.

Judy nodded. "I think so. Let's see here … I put flyers for Coastal Jewels at the Seahorse Inn, Donna's Restaurant, Heirloom, the Book Nook, and at a bunch of other spots around Cape May. I'm trying to spread the word for Tammy. We need to drum up business."

"Well, I hope it works. Where to next?" Bob asked as he put the car in drive.

"Head home. I'm going to call Margaret in the meantime," Judy said as she pulled out her phone and started dialing.

"Hi, Mom," Margaret answered.

"Hi there. I was just curious how you made out with teaching Tammy about starting a business page on social media?" Judy asked as Bob turned towards Beach Avenue.

"Oh, I didn't tell you? It went great. She stopped by Liz's with her laptop and even brought the baby with her. The retreat ladies were just in love, each taking turns holding and playing with little Francine. It gave us a good bit of time to go over everything. Anyway, she's all set up on a few social media platforms. She already posted photos, and I believe posted an event," Margaret said as she walked through the woods.

"Really? What kind of event?" Judy asked.

"You know, I'm not exactly sure. I know she's holding a sale and adding in some other fun things. It sounded nice," Margaret said as a crow squawked in the background.

"Where are you?" Judy asked.

"Pinetree Wildlife Refuge. I came to bring Dave his lunch that he left at the house. I haven't been back here much since I started working from home. I forgot how much I love it here," Margaret said as she stared up at the canopy of pine trees above her.

"Well, maybe you can stop in more often … or start working there once a week," Judy said as Bob pulled the car into the driveway.

"Oh, no. I prefer to work from home. It's makes it easier for me to manage all my businesses."

Judy shook her head and laughed. "What is it now? The Seahorse Inn, the Tea Garden, and now the Beach House Market on top of working for the refuge?"

Margaret shrugged as she watched Dave walking towards her with a big smile. "I know. I know. I have too many things going on, but the tea garden is not a steady gig. It's just a here-and-there reservation type thing. The Beach House Market is self-running so far, and the Seahorse Inn has great employees that keep it running for Liz and me. It all works out so well. I better go, though. I just found Dave."

"OK, well, tell him we say hello. We'll talk later," Judy said as she hung up.

Dave kissed Margaret on the cheek as she handed him his lunch bag. "I thought you'd need this today. I brought my own if you want to eat together on the picnic table."

"Sounds perfect. I can't thank you enough for bringing it. I was so looking forward to the sandwich I made and that pasta salad you whipped up," Dave said as he took a seat with Margaret at the table.

"I also made myself the same sandwich. When I saw you making it this morning, I knew I needed one. Pesto, fresh mozzarella, prosciutto, arugula, olive oil, and balsamic glaze. Seriously, it's a dream," she said while unwrapping her sandwich then took a bite.

Dave pulled out his phone. "So, the bay house is listed online already."

Margaret widened her eyes. "Already?"

Dave shrugged and smiled. "Looks like we've got ourselves a good realtor so far. She definitely gets things done quickly. Here, take a look at the listing," he said, pushing the phone towards her.

Margaret picked up the phone and scrolled through the photos. "Wow. Ben really does know what he's doing. These pictures look great."

Dave nodded. "They do. The description is great too. She texted me and said that an hour after the listing went up, she received multiple requests for showings. So buckle up. I have a feeling things are about to go into turbo mode."

* * *

That evening over on the harbor, Chris and Sarah sat on the third-level deck, admiring the boats as well as the stars and moon above them.

"This is literally a dream. I can't believe we get to live here," Chris said as he sighed and leaned back in his chair.

Sarah nodded. "I love that you can hear the shorebirds and the frogs. It's so quiet and peaceful aside from a passing boat here and there, but I enjoy those sounds too. I could even do yoga out here before bed," she said, feeling full of hope and excitement.

Chris smiled and closed his eyes as he took a deep breath, savoring the peace all around them, when a loud bang from across the street startled them.

"What was that?" Sarah asked, sitting up in her chair.

They both paused for a moment, and there it was. A band out on the deck of a nearby restaurant had started up for the evening, and the noise echoed off the houses.

Chris furrowed his brow. "Uh, I guess we get free live entertainment now?"

Sarah bit her lip. "Well, that peace and quiet was short-lived. I hope this isn't all weekend."

Their neighbors next door went out onto their deck, stared over at the restaurant with the band, then turned to see Chris and Sarah. "Hello, new neighbors! We finally meet. This is Tim, and I'm Erin," Erin yelled over the music.

Chris and Sarah stood up. "Great to meet you guys. We absolutely love it here. We moved from North Cape May by the bay."

Tim nodded. "Well, welcome to our beloved harbor community. As you can see, we even get our own cover band. Hope you like Mötley Crüe blaring until the wee hours."

"Is it … all weekend?" Sarah asked hesitantly.

Erin rolled her eyes. "Unfortunately. It's been going on for a couple years now. A lot of us in the community have raised concerns about it, even talking with the managers of the restaurant, but nothing has changed. If you want a peaceful weekend here, it's going to have to be in the offseason."

Tim stared towards the restaurant. "As much as we love living here, I'm ready to move. It feels like we live above a bar the way the noise echoes out here."

"There's got to be some kind of compromise with this restaurant," Chris said, suddenly feeling a little worried about their decision to move from their quiet bay house.

"We've tried, and multiple other neighbors have tried. We don't know what else we can do at this point. Well, we're heading out. It was nice to meet you two. We'll catch up next time," Erin said as she and Tim walked back inside.

Sarah looked over at Chris with worry all over her face. "We have to do something."

CHAPTER NINE

Lisa and Nick walked through the Cape May Point State Park trails the next morning. Lisa stopped to admire some white rose mallows blooming on either side of the boardwalk.

"They're pretty, aren't they?" Nick asked as he smiled at Lisa.

Lisa nodded, trying to force a smile back. "They are, and they're everywhere."

"Oh, look. There's a frog on that tree," Nick said, pointing. "I heard some frogs near my house yesterday. They were loud."

Lisa didn't look at the frog. Instead she looked up at the sky then back at Nick. "Nick, we have to talk."

"Sure, go ahead," Nick said as he put his hands in his pockets.

Lisa felt her stomach turn. She didn't want to confront Nick, but she had to. "Why haven't you shown me your house yet? We've been dating long enough now, plus you've seen my place."

Nick took a deep breath. "Well, we've already talked about this. I'm getting work done on my place. It's just a huge mess. I don't want you stepping on any nails or loose boards."

Lisa shifted her eyes. "I guess I'm not understanding why

you've never even driven me by your house just to see where it is …"

Nick paused in thought. "The roof is all torn up while it's getting replaced. It's just ugly. The yard is trashed. I don't want you to see it that way."

Lisa was sick to her stomach, but she ignored that and looked Nick straight in the eyes. "You live on Missouri Avenue, correct?"

Nick's face turned white. "Yes … I do, but … how do you …"

Lisa crossed her arms. "Nick, I've seen your house. It's not under construction. The roof is not getting repaired, and the yard looks perfectly manicured. In fact, there's two older people that seem to be living in it."

"You drove by my house? So you basically spied on me," Nick said, suddenly becoming defensive.

Lisa felt steam coming out of her ears. "Spying on you? Please. Donna and I drove by the other day just to see what your house looked like. It's not a mystery. Your address comes right up on the internet. It's a little weird to be dating someone that's so secretive about where they live, I must say. Now I know you're a liar, though, just like my ex-husband."

"Did you stake out where he was too?" Nick asked.

Lisa felt tears welling up in her eyes. "Actually, Nick, as you may remember me telling you, he had a whole other family that he kept secret from me. A girlfriend, kids, all of that. I found out while driving to the other side of the island for work. I stopped somewhere to get lunch, and while I sat in a booth by myself, he walked in with his other family. He was holding his new baby and everything. I was so devastated that I slinked down into the booth and froze. I couldn't get up, move, leave, nothing."

Nick sat down on a bench and threw his head into his hands. He then sat up and wiped away some tears from his eyes. "I'm sorry, Lisa. I'm an idiot. I don't know why I've been so secretive about my house …. You know, yes I do. Those people living there are my parents."

"So it's their house? You live with your parents?" Lisa asked, still standing in front of Nick.

Nick shook his head. "No. They live with me. They couldn't afford their house any longer. They could barely afford groceries. I moved them in with me a year ago. I love them, but they drive me nuts. The past year has been hard, to say the least. There's a lot of bickering between us. None of my other siblings wanted to help out because they don't get along with them. So it was me or they would be in a bad situation. I couldn't let that happen."

Lisa took a deep breath and sat next to Nick. "So why couldn't you just tell me that? I guess that's the part I'm not understanding. To start a relationship with crazy lies is insane!"

"I know it is. I panicked. I didn't want you to know that I lived with my parents initially when we first met. Then it just spiraled from there," Nick said, staring at the ground.

"But you don't 'live with your parents.' *They* live with *you*. That's a big difference," Lisa said. She wanted to pat his shoulder or even touch his hand, but a part of her was still repulsed that he would lie about something like this.

Nick turned to look at Lisa. "It was just that. I feared the day you would have to meet them. There's a reason my siblings don't talk to them. They weren't exactly good parents to us growing up, and they still have their issues now. I just didn't want you anywhere near my house."

"How bad could they possibly be?" Lisa asked as she watched some people walk by them on the trail.

"My dad was a drunk, and you could tell my mom just never wanted kids. She must have felt obligated to have us because she always made it seem like a chore to do anything with us. As soon as we were old enough to be home alone, she would come home from work and immediately leave the house, not coming home until well after our bedtime. My dad would just sit in the living room, pounding a bottle of alcohol, and me and my siblings had to make our own dinners every night. Let's just say we ate a lot of macaroni and cheese with hot dogs and soda. We didn't have those wonderful homemade meals you saw the other parents cooking. Neither of them made much of an effort to come to our sporting events or anything else." Nick looked off into the distance. "Then there's now. I'm miserable living with them. They're still very selfish people, but I love them. I only want the best for them. So I'm probably going to let them live in my house, and I'm going to move out to somewhere new. It's why I've been at your place so much lately. The good thing is I'm doing well enough with the oyster farm that I should be able to manage paying for two houses. Or maybe I can rent something like you're doing. I know I just need out before I go insane. They've taken over the entire house. I can't even relax and watch a movie in the living room because they're both in there watching *Bonanza* and the news twenty-four seven. It doesn't feel like my house anymore."

"I'm so sorry," Lisa said, feeling tears welling up in her eyes.

Nick took a deep breath, then leaned his head onto Lisa's shoulder. "I'm so sorry for all these stupid lies. I'm so ashamed."

"I mean, it's starting to make more sense why you hid this from me, but yes, I still have an issue with any kind of lies in a relationship," Lisa said as she swatted a bug out of her face.

Nick sat up. "I totally understand. If this is a deal-breaker for us, then I guess I'll just have to live with my mistake, but I don't want it to be. I like you, Lisa … a lot. So much so that I didn't want my parents to get in the way of that."

Lisa sighed. "I get that. I really do, but I still need some time to process all of this."

* * *

"Darlene! Over here!" Susan yelled from the beach as Darlene walked in the opposite direction.

"Where is she *going*?" Samantha asked as she grabbed a drink out of the cooler and took a sip.

Chrissy stood up amongst the group of retreat ladies and waved her hands in the air. "Hey, Darlene!"

Darlene finally turned around, looking quite confused, then spotted the group.

"Finally. I thought she was about to walk three blocks away before we got her attention," Chrissy said as she sat back down in her beach chair.

The group laughed as they relaxed in their chairs under the umbrellas among the crowds of people on the hot beach.

"I was told you all were by the lifeguard stand," Darlene said as she plopped into an empty chair and fanned herself with her hands.

Kristen looked towards the lifeguard stand, which was twenty-five feet away. "Well, we kind of are. Not exactly next to it, though."

"Did anyone bring snacks? I'm starved," Tonya asked as she peeked into the cooler next to her.

Maryanne shook her head. "No, but there is a little place around here that delivers your lunch to the beach. We were thinking about ordering with them."

"Count me in. Is there a menu?" Tonya asked.

"It's going around. Becky has it now. Just write down what you want," Maryanne said as she turned the radio up when some '70s rock song came on.

Kristen glanced around the beach, and her eyes stopped on something in the distance. She lowered her sunglasses to get a better look then turned to the rest of the women. "Did you guys see that group of men over there?"

Tonya turned around in her seat to look. "You talking about those silver-haired foxes by the volleyball net?"

Kristen chuckled. "Yes."

Tonya sat back in her seat. "I saw them as soon as we got on the beach. They've been looking over here at us the entire time."

"Who?" Susan asked loudly, only hearing part of the conversation.

Tonya rolled her eyes. "Those men that look to be around our age sitting over there in a group just like we are. They keep looking over here."

Susan strained her neck to see. "Oh, I see them now. Some of them are quite cute."

"Susan! Don't make it obvious," Maggie said as she lowered her sun hat over her face.

The rest of the group finally caught on to the conversation and turned to look at the men as well.

"I'm married, but I'm rooting for you all. Go over there and strike up a conversation," Chrissy said as she rubbed sunblock on her arms.

Darlene shook her head. "I'm good. I don't need another man to care for. I'll be happily single for the rest of my life."

"Looks like they're throwing a football now," Samantha said as she glanced back at them.

"Why do they keep inching this way?" Maryanne asked.

Susan shrugged. "Probably just need to spread out so they can throw farther."

Maggie laid back in her chair and popped her headphones in. She had just taken a deep breath when *bam!* Sand flew all over her face and into her mouth. She sat up to see a football had landed right next to her.

One of the men throwing the football approached. "Sorry about that, ladies," he said as he knelt down to pick up the ball.

"Oh, that's no problem at all," Tonya said as she stood up to adjust the umbrella.

The man stood there with the football, looking back at his friends. He mouthed something to them, and the next thing they knew, the entire group of men they had been ogling were right next to them.

"Ladies, how's it going?" one of the approaching men asked.

Kristen eyed the men's hands, not noticing wedding rings on any of them. "It's going. Just hanging on the beach. What are you all up to?"

One of the guys raised his hand. "I'm Ted. We're actually having a boys'—I mean *men's*—week. We're staying across the street there at the Sunny Seashell Inn."

"Really? Well, I'm Samantha. Nice to meet you, Ted. We're having a women's week, and we're also staying across the street at an inn. How funny is that?"

"Well, that is funny. This is the first time we've ever done something like this," Ted said as he flashed a smile.

Another one of the men with gray hair and a beard picked up the football and tossed it. "I hate to be too forward, but are you all married? I'm Liam, by the way."

Chrissy raised her hand. "Just me. They're all single and ready to mingle."

A couple of the women gave Chrissy a death stare while the rest of the women and men laughed, which cut the awkwardness.

Tonya held out the lunch menu. "Do you guys want to join us for lunch on the beach? We're about to order."

"I'm starving. We were just talking about lunch. That would be great. We'll head back and get our chairs if that's OK," Liam said.

"Please do!" Darlene yelled to them as they headed across the beach.

Forty-five minutes later, the men had integrated their chairs into the group and lunch had been delivered.

Liam pulled his chair closer to Kristen as he ate his turkey sandwich. "Want some of my chips?"

Kristen nodded. "Salt and vinegar chips? Oh yes, that's my absolute favorite," she said as she dug her hand into the bag.

"A girl after my own heart," Liam said then smiled. "How is your week at the Jersey shore going so far?"

"It's been wonderful. We've been to some wineries, went swimming in a pool a few times, went out to eat, shopping, boating, and plenty of beach time, of course. What about you?"

"There's been a lot of trail walking and eating, I can tell you that. This is our first time on the beach since we got here. I didn't think we'd actually make it," Liam said with a chuckle.

"Oh? Why's that?" Kristen asked as she ate a chip.

"Not all the guys here were keen to sit on the beach. They get bored easily. That's why they wanted to throw around a football. Me? I could sit out here all day and let my worries drift away."

"Same here," Kristen said as she smiled and nudged Liam.

"Where are you from?" Liam asked.

"I live in Massachusetts. Specifically, Yarmouth, Massachusetts. You?"

Liam's mouth dropped open. "Are you being serious right now?"

"Of course," Kristen said as she turned to Liam, but not before noticing all the other conversations going on in the group. It appeared each of the men and women were getting along and enjoying themselves.

"This is going to sound crazy, but I'm moving to Yarmouth next month. I just got a job there. Currently, I'm in upstate New York. How coincidental is this?" Liam asked.

Kristen smiled. "Very … well, I can show you around. It's a great place."

Liam took a deep breath. "I'd like that. Maybe I can take you out to dinner sometime too."

"That could definitely be arranged."

Liam took out his phone and smiled. "I'm thinking we should swap numbers now. What do you say?"

CHAPTER TEN

"Thank you for coming in today. I really appreciate it," Tammy said as she placed chocolate chip cookies on a tray.

Judy smiled and repositioned some necklaces for sale. "I'm glad to be here for your first event at Coastal Jewels. It's nothing, really."

Tammy sighed. "I hope it goes well. There seemed to be a lot of interest in the event I created online, but who's to say if anyone actually comes."

Judy put out some paper cups with lemonade and iced tea pitchers on the table beside the cookies, vegetables, dips, and sandwiches. "Well, between all of the flyers I handed out and your new social media page, I'm crossing my fingers that there's a nice turnout."

Tammy looked out the big front window. "It's so weird to be able to finally see the street since the landlord trimmed the bushes way down, and the new sign, it's gorgeous with all of the painted flowers around the edges, isn't it?"

Judy nodded. "It is. I'm glad Margaret got Liz to whip that up for you. Liz is quite creative, I'll say that."

Tammy walked behind the counter and turned the upbeat

music up, then she opened the door. "Going to let some fresh air in. It's such a beautiful day."

Moments later, a car pulled up in the driveway and out came two women, who then walked inside.

"My gosh, I didn't even know this store was here. Look how lovely it is, Gretchen," the woman said to her friend as she took off her sunglasses.

Gretchen's eyes widened as she stood near the doorway. "I've been searching for the perfect jewelry store, Patty. This might be it."

Tammy smiled then pointed to the table across the room. "We're having a sale today. Twenty percent off on select pieces, and please help yourself to any of the drinks or snacks."

"Say no more. I love a good sip-and-mingle event," Patty said as she picked up a cup and poured some lemonade in it.

Tammy glanced at Patty. "Sip and Mingle. I think you just named my future events here. I love the sound of that."

"I'm glad to help," Patty said with a smile as she walked around the shop with Gretchen and their drinks.

Tammy walked behind the counter with Judy. "Well, that's two more than we usually get here. I'd call this day a win."

Judy smiled. "It definitely is a win," she said as she glanced around. "Look at how cutting back those bushes in the front let in so much more light. The crystals and stones on the jewelry are shimmering now."

"Oh my gosh, you're right. It looks like there's sparkling glitter in the air," Tammy said in awe as she looked around the room.

Judy turned to the back door, noticing more cars pulling up. "Don't look now, but I think we're about to get more than two customers today."

Three more cars pulled up with a total of six women, then a fourth and fifth car with even more women.

"I'm going to scream," Tammy said as she tried not to

jump up and down. "Look at all these people coming into the store. I'm amazed."

They greeted the new customers, and the little store was becoming packed with people.

Gretchen walked up to the counter with two necklaces, a bracelet, and a ring. "I think I'm ready to check out."

"Me, too," Patty said as she set a bracelet on the counter. "Though it looks like we picked a good time to leave. There's a big group about to come inside," she said, looking out the back door.

Judy turned around to see Dolly, Kim, Margaret and the Seahorse Inn women's retreat ladies walking inside. "Look who's here," she said happily.

Tonya's bangles on her wrist clinked as she reached up to look at a long beaded necklace. "Oh, this is right up my alley."

Margaret squeezed in next to the counter in the packed store. "This is a great turnout."

Tammy smiled from ear to ear as she handed a customer her change. "It really is. I can't thank you and Liz enough for helping me with the sign and the social media page. And, Judy, I, of course, will never be able to repay you for all of your help."

"It was nothing. We were glad to help," Margaret said as she watched the retreat ladies mingling and shopping in the store. "What are your plans from here?"

Tammy closed the register and turned to Margaret. "Well, I've started signing up for some local festivals and craft fairs, and I'm planning to have more of these sip-and-mingle events for sure. I think I'm going to be OK. At least it feels that way right now."

"That's wonderful. So glad to hear that. We want our local businesses to thrive here in Cape May," Margaret said just as Tonya laid five beaded necklaces on the counter.

"These match perfectly with my bangles. I need them all,"

Tonya said as she pulled out her wallet. "I have a problem," she said while chuckling.

"Yes, you do." Susan laughed as she waited in line behind her.

* * *

"Are you sure you want to go inside?" Nick asked hesitantly as he and Lisa sat in his car.

"Yes. Why? Do you think it's too soon for me to meet your parents?" Lisa asked.

"Oh, no. That's not what I meant. They're not the easiest to get along with. That's all. I guess I'm worried that this could go badly."

Lisa shrugged. "You've already told me everything about them, so I know what to expect. Plus, I'm used to dealing with difficult people. My ex-in-laws were awful."

"Really? How so?" Nick asked.

"They knew about my ex's other family the whole time we were married. I found this out afterwards. On top of that, they were never nice to me and never showed any interest in me. Then his mom had the audacity to call me after the divorce and tell me they were disappointed in me for leaving their son."

Nick shifted his eyes. "What? Am I hearing this correctly? Their son cheated on you, and they were mad that you left him?"

Lisa nodded. "Basically. His mom and I got into it over the phone, but I started to piece together that his father did the same thing to her. She must've thought I should've stayed just like she did with her horrendous marriage."

Nick shook his head. "I feel terrible."

"Don't. It's over, and I'm much happier now. I don't even really want to look back on any of that anymore."

"I know. I just feel bad that you now have to deal with my

parents after dealing with that," Nick said as he stared towards the front door.

Lisa put her hand on Nick's. "It's fine. Really."

"OK, but I just have to warn you, they also have a problem with collecting too much stuff," Nick said as he opened the door.

Lisa laughed. "Don't we all collect things?"

Nick gave Lisa a look as they approached the front door, and as they stepped inside, Lisa suddenly understood that his parents were hoarders.

"Do you see what I mean?" Nick said as he pointed to the piles and piles of magazines and newspapers on every surface.

Lisa widened her eyes in disbelief. She'd seen TV shows about hoarders, but she'd never seen it up close like this. The sitting room they walked into didn't have anywhere to sit as it was piled up with stuff. The coffee table didn't have an inch of surface to put a cup on, as it was piled high with more things. Even the window ledges were jammed with empty bottles.

"This is one of the many other reasons I didn't want you to see my house. I've been throwing their 'stuff' out as much as I can without them knowing, but they just keep adding to it when I'm not home. It's become a full-time job," Nick said as he looked towards the living room. "They're in there watching TV. They probably don't even know we're here yet. That's how loud the TV always is."

Lisa nodded and followed Dave into the living room. His parents, Joan and Dennis, looked up from their recliners as Lisa smiled and waved.

"This is Lisa!" Nick yelled over the television.

"Huh?" Joan asked as she held her hand up to her ear.

"He said Lisa!" Dennis yelled.

Nick rolled his eyes. "Turn the television down for a minute, please."

"Oh, right ..." Dennis said as he searched for the remote, finally turning it down.

"I was saying this is Lisa," Nick said as he turned to Lisa. "And this is my mom and dad, Joan and Dennis."

"Nice to meet you two," Lisa said as she smiled. "You're watching *Bonanza*? Such a great show."

"It is," Joan said, nodding. "Uh, Nick ... is this a new girl-friend again?"

Nick felt the blood drain from his face. "Um, Mom, what do you mean *again*?"

"I mean *again*. It feels like yesterday you introduced us to some other girl. What was her name? Oh, Leslie. What ever happened to her?" Joan asked.

Dennis shook his head, frustrated. "Joan, that was years ago. Don't you remember?"

Joan paused for a moment in thought. "I could have sworn it was not too long ago."

Dennis glanced at Nick. "I told you her memory is going. We need to get her to a doctor."

Joan squinted at Dennis. "I'm sitting right here. Why are you talking about me like I'm not in the room?"

Dennis sat up in his recliner. "Because you don't listen to me when I tell you about your memory issues. You just blow me off. At least Nick will listen."

Lisa spoke up quickly to break the awkwardness. "I get my dates mixed up all the time. Some things feel so long ago, and others feel like they happened just the other day, right?"

Nick delicately touched Lisa's back and took a deep breath. "Right. It happens, but it can't hurt to get you checked out, Mom. We'll schedule you an appointment."

Joan rolled her eyes. "I'm sick of everyone telling me what to do and how I'm acting. I think I know myself."

Nick nodded to move on from the subject as the tension was getting to be too much in the room. "I'm going to show Lisa the rest of the house and then we're headed out. Are you two otherwise OK?"

"We're fine. We're having leftovers for dinner," Dennis said as he turned the volume on the TV back up to blaring.

Nick guided Lisa into the kitchen by her hand. "I'm so sorry. Do you see what I'm talking about?" he whispered.

Lisa nodded. "Yes, I get it," she said as she looked around the kitchen. There wasn't an inch of counter space due to boxes and cans of food sitting all over it. She looked at Nick, wanting to say more to comfort him, but was afraid his parents in the next room would overhear.

"Even the kitchen hasn't escaped their stuff. They packed my pantry full, and whatever couldn't fit now sits on the counters," Nick said as he looked around the room in disgust. "I guess I'll show you the bedrooms, even though I'm hesitant," he said while leading her down the hall.

"There're three bedrooms. This one is mine," he said, opening the door to the cleanest room in the house. "I guess I'm a bit of a minimalist, or maybe being around my parents pushed me into being that way," he said with a chuckle.

"I'm impressed," Lisa said as she walked around the room, noticing the perfectly made king-sized bed with two matching end tables and lamps. "It looks super cozy."

Nick nodded. "This room's become my sanctuary, so I invested in the softest sheets and a quality comforter and duvet. This is definitely coming with me when I move, that's for sure," he said as he looked towards the door. "I don't want to show you the other two rooms. My parents stay in those, separately, and that's their space, but come check out the backyard," he said as they walked towards the kitchen and out the back door.

They stepped outside onto a stamped concrete patio bordered by thick, lush green grass.

"It's beautiful out here," Lisa said, admiring how perfectly manicured the bushes, trees, and grass seemed to be.

Nick smiled. "I want to show you something," he said, leading her to a small wooden shed. He opened the doors to a gutted space. There weren't any yard care tools in sight, but instead there was a small black-and-white television in the corner and a cutting-board counter with a couple vintage lawn chairs.

"What is this? A man cave?" Lisa asked as she looked around.

Nick shrugged. "You could say that. Sometimes I bring oysters from the farm back here and shuck them. Usually, I'll have some buddies over, and we'll put the game on the TV. We'll have some beers and oysters and hang out here for hours. Besides my room, this is the only part of my home that's given me sanity since my parents moved in."

Lisa smiled. "I love this for you. I hope you get something similar at the new place."

Nick walked out of the shed with Lisa and closed the doors. "Here's hoping. Well, I think I've showed you everything I can about the house. I'm not taking you to the bathrooms. I'm afraid of what we may see. Let's just say goodbye and head out," Nick said as they walked back inside and through the living room.

"It was nice to you meet you two," Lisa said to Joan and Dennis over the blaring TV.

Dennis waved, not taking his eyes off the television, and Joan mumbled something as she adjusted herself in her chair.

"I'll see you guys later. Call me if you need anything," Nick said as he led Lisa out of the house and back to the car.

They both got in the car, and Nick turned the ignition then leaned his head back on the headrest. "That was a nightmare. An absolute nightmare. I see more and more why my siblings want nothing to do with them."

Lisa put her hand on Nick's shoulder. "Nobody's family is perfect. Nobody. Even the ones that seem perfect have their issues. However, I do think getting your own place is definitely the answer here."

Nick sighed as he put his hand on Lisa's. "Thank you for understanding, and yes, I need to find my own place stat. I'd like to get something closer to the oyster farm, but at this point, it doesn't matter where it is."

"I'll help you find something. We can make it fun, like finding a diamond in the rough," Lisa said with a smile.

Nick smiled back at Lisa. "I would like that. You can help me furnish and decorate, too, if you'd like. I'm not good at that stuff."

"Sure. Whatever you want," Lisa said as Nick put the car into drive.

CHAPTER ELEVEN

Dave felt his phone ring as he walked around Pinetree Wildlife Refuge.

"Hey, Melissa. How's it going?" Dave answered.

Melissa smiled. "It's going really well. I called to let you know there's a bit of a bidding war going on with your bay house."

"Really? That's exciting," Dave said as he hopped into his truck.

"It is, indeed. I knew your place would be highly coveted. It has a lot of things that people look for when purchasing a home. I'm putting a deadline for the buyers to put their highest offer in by next week, and then we can go over everything and decide on a potential buyer for the house."

"Perfect. Thank you so much, Melissa. Talk to you soon," Dave said as he hung up and called Margaret.

"Hey, how's it going over at the refuge?" Margaret answered.

Dave nodded happily. "It's great. We've got a boatload of volunteers lately, and the refuge looks pristine. Peter and I have started creating trails throughout the woods behind the buildings. The education center wants to do some moonlight frog walks with the public, among other things."

"That sounds great. I'd like to join one of those," Margaret said as she walked around the outside of Liz's garage workshop.

"Same. By the way, I have good news. Well, first is I'm done at the refuge for the day. Peter and I got covered in ticks while creating part of the trail. We both didn't dress and prepare for being out in the woods. We didn't have any tick repellant on and wore shorts and short-sleeve shirts. A big no-no, apparently. We need breathable long-sleeved shirts and long pants with tall socks and hats.

"The other good news is the bay house is probably going to be sold pretty soon. Melissa called and said there's a bidding war going on. I don't know how many people it's between, but she is going to give a deadline for the bidders to put in their highest offer. Then we'll decide on who the buyer will be."

"Gosh, that's so exciting. It sounds like it could go for a pretty penny after all of this," Margaret said. "By the way, I'm at Liz and Greg's, out in Liz's workshop. You should see the stuff she's working on. She restored this incredible dining room table set. It sold for six thousand dollars. I'm helping her load it into the buyer's van since Greg won't be home in time to help."

"Well, call me if you need me. I'm going to take a drive. Possibly stop at some garden nurseries and maybe get some seeds for fall crops," Dave said as he started up the truck.

Margaret smiled. "Ah, yes. We should probably start thinking about what we're going to sell in the fall at the Beach House Market. I'm picturing pumpkins and gourds—"

Dave nodded. "It's a good thing we decided to plant that big pumpkin patch this year, but now is a good time to get the rest of the fall crops planted."

"OK, call me later. It looks the buyer is here and ready to load the table up. Oh, by the way, can you do me a favor and stop by the Seahorse later? The oven you fixed is acting up again. It's not a rush, though. We still have the other working oven."

"That ol' oven again. It may be time to get a new one, but I'll have a look," Dave said.

Margaret sighed. "I know. We probably should just get a new one. Irene is there, and she'll show you the issue. Thank you so much. You're the best. I'll call when I'm on my way home," she said, then they both said their goodbyes and hung up.

Dave drove the truck out towards Cape May, taking back roads until he got to Beach Avenue. He followed it down towards the Seahorse, where he then approached a roadblock.

"What is going on here?" he asked out loud, noticing a detour sign with traffic being diverted up the street.

He followed the detour signs initially but decided to turn away from the cars he was following and somehow made his way onto a small one-way alley two blocks from the beach. He slowed the truck down and looked around. In all his years living in Cape May, he had never been on this street. It appeared to be mostly driveways of houses that faced the street behind it. However, there, hidden in the midst of all that, was a small, weathered, wood-sided cottage under big shady oak and maple trees. It had a screened-in porch just like the bay house, and a small hand-written For Sale sign that Dave had to squint to see from the street. He immediately pulled the truck over in front of the house and got out. He started taking pictures until he noticed an older gentleman in a rocking chair on the porch.

"Hi, there. Can I help you?" the man asked as he rocked back and forth with his radio playing softly.

Dave put his phone down and pointed to the For Sale sign. "I just happened to be driving by and saw your sign. Thought I'd take photos to show my wife."

The man nodded. "That sign went up this morning. You're the first person I've seen stop and look."

"It's a nice home. We're in the process of selling our bay

house over in North Cape May. I just happened to be in the area due to that detour over on Beach Avenue. I never even knew this street was here."

"Nobody does. I like it that way. Keeps it nice and quiet. You're welcome to come up onto the porch and have a look," the man said, pointing to the old paint-chipped screen door.

"That'd be great," Dave said as he walked up the cracked front steps and onto the porch. "I'm Dave," he said, extending his hand.

"Howard," the man said as his frail hand shook Dave's. "Take a seat for a moment."

Dave sat in the rocking chair next to Howard and looked around. It was obvious parts of the home hadn't been kept up with for years, but it was charming nonetheless with a couple vintage glass lamps sitting on a table next to the chairs.

"My wife and I lived here for fifty years. Raised our children and everything. She passed six months ago, and now feels like the right time to sell. My kids live all over the country, but my daughter wants me to move in with her family in Florida. She thinks the warm weather will be good for me. Plus, she's a natural caretaker—a nurse, after all. I don't want to leave, but I know she's right. I'm almost ninety."

"I get it. My parents left here and moved to Florida to escape the winters. I, on the other hand, don't see myself ever leaving," Dave said with a chuckle.

Howard laughed. "I like your fighting spirit. Did you want to see the house?" he said as he shakily got up out of the rocking chair.

"That would be great if you don't mind," Dave said as he followed him inside.

Once inside, Dave immediately fell in love. The house looked like it hadn't been updated since the 1990s. It was the perfect canvas for Dave to build upon in an amazing location, but his heart sank a little as Howard showed him around. How would Howard feel about someone buying the house he loved so dearly and remodeling it?

"It needs to be remodeled," Howard said, jolting Dave out of his thoughts.

"What was that?" Dave asked, making sure he heard what he thought he did.

"This house needs a lot of work. Over the years, my wife and I kind of stopped worrying about updates. We spent more time and money hanging with our family. You know, making memories baking in the kitchen, running the sprinkler in the backyard for the kids to play in, taking walks to get ice cream, sitting on the porch telling stories and playing board games, taking them camping and to Disney World. Now that I look back, I'm glad we did, because my wife, Pat, was never happier than when she was surrounded by family," Howard said as he looked around the living room.

Dave nodded. "Totally understandable. Time with loved ones doesn't compare to anything else. I can tell this home has good bones, and I love the vintage charm. The stained-glass window going up the stairs is gorgeous," Dave said, pointing.

"We've always loved that. When the sun comes through, it projects the different colors onto the walls. There's more throughout the house," Howard said, smiling. "You'll have to see it."

Howard led Dave through the kitchen, the basement, the bathrooms, and even the upstairs. It was evident the house needed a lot of work, just like Howard had mentioned and Dave had suspected.

"Before you go, I want to show you the yard. It's probably my favorite part," Howard said, leading Dave out the front door.

Dave and Howard walked around the side of the house until they came to the large backyard full of more shady trees and lush green grass with plenty of shrubs bordering the fence line.

"It's nice out here," Dave said, looking around.

Howard waved his hand in the air. "This is not even the part that's my favorite. Follow me this way," he said, walking towards the shrubs near the back of the property. As they got closer, Dave could see an opening in the shrubs that led to a gravel pathway.

"This here is our access to the beach. Nobody really knows about it except our neighbors around us. Plus, the public can't access it since you can only get to it from private property. You'll cross over one street, and then it puts you out on Beach Avenue."

"How cool is that?" Dave said as he peeked down the trail.

Howard pointed ahead. "Go walk down it and come back so you can see. I'll wait right here."

"I think I will," Dave said as he headed off down the trail. He walked one block, crossed over a street and continued onto the path in between houses until he came to Beach Avenue. He looked to his left and laughed. The Seahorse Inn was only a few houses down from the path. He thought about running over to check on the oven, but he didn't want to keep Howard waiting, so he headed back.

"What did you think?" Howard asked excitedly.

Dave smiled. "I think that's super cool. Also, the path stops right near a bed-and-breakfast that my wife runs with her sister. The Seahorse Inn."

"Really? That big blue inn there? It's run by your wife?" Howard asked.

"Yes, it got handed down through the family. I helped restore it, and she and her sister reopened it for bookings," Dave said.

Howard started walking back towards the house, with Dave following behind. "So, you're good at restoring things?"

Dave nodded. "Yes, and remodeling. Now that we're selling the bay house, I just started looking for a fixer-upper. I'd like a little beach house near the ocean we can stay in with family. I just love building. It's what's I'm good at."

Howard pointed to the house. "I've got your fixer-upper right here for you."

"Really? You're OK if I took down some walls, put in a new kitchen and bathrooms, and possibly put on an addition?" Dave asked.

Howard shrugged. "Why not? It's not like you'd be knocking the house down. I'd love to see it last many more years."

Dave smiled, feeling excitement building up. "I'll have to talk to the wife, and we need to sell our other house, though that seems it will happen soon, my realtor tells me."

"Of course. We'll discuss price and all of that. I'll let you have first dibs, but I do have to talk to my kids to let them know what's going on. Take down my phone number so you have it," Howard said as Dave pulled out his cell phone and plugged in his number.

* * *

"Where did you get these pies?" Chris asked as he and Sarah walked across the street to Fish 'n' Stuff restaurant.

"Duckie's Farm Market. They're known for their amazing key lime pies. I always give these as a gift when I'm trying to make a good impression," Sarah said as she walked with the boxed pies in her arms.

They got to the front door and walked inside to an empty restaurant.

"I guess the dinner rush hasn't started yet?" Sarah asked as she looked around.

"Table for two?" the host asked as she approached the front stand.

Chris shook his head. "No, we just came in to talk to the manager."

The host nodded. "Well, our manager isn't in yet, but would you like to talk to the owner instead? Dana only pops in once in a while, but you came at a good time. She just got here."

"That'd be great," Sarah said, still holding the pies.

"I'll go get her," the host said as she hurried back towards the kitchen.

Minutes later, out walked a short stocky woman with curly cropped hair. "Hi, there. Did you need me for something?" Dana asked.

Sarah handed her the pies. "Actually, yes. These are for you. Key lime pies from Duckie's."

Dana nodded. "Why … thank you. Mind if I give them to our hard-working kitchen staff? They'll probably devour them right now."

"Sure, that'd be great," Sarah said as she looked around the restaurant nervously.

Dana handed the pies off to the host and crossed her arms. "What are you really here for? I can tell you have something on your mind."

Chris cleared his throat. "We just moved into a home across the street on the harbor. We've learned that the band you hired that plays outside over the weekend in the summer is crazy loud. The noise just bounces off all the houses. Apparently, our neighbors have been dealing with this for years. They've tried to get the band moved inside to no avail."

"They have?" Dana asked as she scratched her head. "I've never heard any complaints before," she said as the host walked to the host stand. Dana turned to the host. "Have you heard about any issues with the band's noise level outside?"

The host nodded. "Yes, I have. I've seen Calvin speaking with some people about it before."

"And nothing was done?" Dana asked, appalled.

The host shrugged. "I don't know what he said to them."

Dana shook her head. "Well, he certainly didn't change

anything. I'm surprised the cops haven't been called yet." Dana turned to Chris. "This has been an issue for years, you said?"

"That's what the neighbor told us."

"Well, since Calvin can't take care of things, I will. We'll move them inside. We already have a stage in here for the band, anyway. It's an easy transition," Dana said, pointing to the back of the restaurant.

"Really?" Sarah asked, completely shocked. "We thought we were going to have to beg and bribe our way to getting anything done."

Dana laughed. "The kitchen will never turn down some key lime pies if you ever have any extra, but no, in all seriousness, I apologize that this hasn't been handled properly. I'll have a talk with Calvin when he comes in later."

CHAPTER TWELVE

The next morning, through a dense fog, Dave and Margaret stocked up on produce and flowers from the gardens for the farm stand.

"I'm going to head down to the market," Margaret yelled to Dave as she passed by him with arms full of sunflowers.

"Hold up. I'll join you," Dave said as he appeared through the fog with a cardboard box loaded with ripe red tomatoes.

Margaret laughed. "It was like a scene out of a movie watching you come out of the garden. The fog is so dense I couldn't see you at first."

Dave nodded as he grasped the box with both hands. "It is pretty neat, isn't it? We don't usually have this kind of fog over our land."

They had started walking through the green grass towards the market when suddenly the fog dissipated and the sun came out from behind some clouds.

As they started getting closer to the market, Margaret stopped walking and scanned the area. "Do you see that? Everything looks like it's been sprinkled with glitter. It's gorgeous."

Dave glanced around. "It does. It must be the sun hitting

the condensation on everything, perhaps? Maybe that's what's causing everything to sparkle."

Margaret nodded, feeling enamored with nature just as a car pulled up on the street in front of the stand. "Looks like we have our first customer of the day. We need to get the doors open," she said, hurrying towards the market.

"Morning. You got here at the perfect time. We were just about to open up for the day," Dave said to the lady as he set the box of tomatoes down and opened up the doors.

"Perfect. We're going to the beach, and I wanted to get some fresh Jersey tomatoes for my homemade tomato pies for dinner. It'll be my grandkids' first time trying these pies. I have to make sure it's only top-notch ingredients."

Margaret smiled as she tucked the fresh sunflower stalks into the tubs of water. "You came to the right spot. We have tons of tomatoes," she said, pointing to a shelf.

As Dave placed the newly picked tomatoes out for customers, another car pulled up. This time, a couple who had their golden retriever with them stepped out.

"Hi, there," Margaret said as the couple approached, staring at everything.

"Oh, hi. We were just driving by and thought we'd check this out. Do you grow all of this?" the man asked.

Margaret nodded. "We do. We have a bunch of big gardens up the hill by our house."

"Wow. This is impressive," the man said as he let their dog smell the different areas out front of the market while his wife walked around inside.

Moments later, another car pulled up, then another and another.

Harper and Abby walked down from the house, wearing bathing suits and goggles on their heads. "I thought we were heading out to go swimming?" Harper asked as she looked around at the bustling activity at the market.

Margaret shrugged as she gave a customer some change.

"We will still go, but first, how would you two like to help bag items for the customers? I've got a lady here with four zucchinis that need to go in one of the paper bags."

"I've got it," Abby said as she flung the bag open and quickly placed the zucchinis into it. "Here you go, ma'am," she said, handing it off to the lady.

Margaret laughed. "Well, well, well. If you keep that up, we might have to pay you for your service."

Harper put her hand on her hip. "Give me a bag. I'm ready for the next customer. Plus, I need some cash."

As more customers poured into the market, Dave, Margaret, and the girls stayed to help make change and bag items, even though it was supposed to be an honor system market.

Judy walked in with her mouth open as she watched Dave stock the shelves and Margaret collecting cash from a line of people. "My goodness. You guys are busy. I guess we're going swimming later, huh?"

Abby nodded and handed Judy some paper bags. "Yes, we're too busy to leave. Help us bag some things."

Margaret shook her head and laughed. "You don't have to help, Mom, but yes, our plans today have been pushed back just a little."

"Please, I'd love to help," Judy said as she held the bags.

Margaret waved her over. "Well, come over here and help some customers. The list of prices of everything is on the wall here," she said, pointing. "I'm going to direct the cars to park up on the grass in front of the market. The street is getting too congested."

Moments later, Liz, Greg, and their boys pulled up, and Margaret waved them over to a spot on the grass to park.

Liz stepped out of the car and lowered her sunglasses. "This is the 'little' produce stand business?" she asked, laughing. "You've got a full-fledged bustling farmers market."

Greg nodded as the boys walked into the market, wearing

their bathing suits. "We were going to park in the driveway but decided to see what all the commotion was first."

Margaret smiled. "It's the busiest I've ever seen it, and yes, we're still going to the water park in Wildwood. Just have to get through this mad rush first. I'm directing the new customers to park on the grass."

"I can do that," Greg said. "Go do what you have to do."

"Thank you," Margaret said as she and Liz walked inside the market, maneuvering around all the customers.

"Margaret, we're almost out of ones, and I need them for some change," Judy said as she held the last dollar bill in the air.

"Oh, boy. Mom, ask them to use a card or a cash app for now," Margaret said as she glanced at Dave.

"I'll go to the bank and get ones," Dave said as he headed towards the driveway.

"Dave!" Greg yelled after him. "I'll take you in my car right here. Dale and Chris are going to help customers park."

Dave turned around. "Dale and Chris are here?" he asked, squinting to see through the sunlight.

"We're here too," Sarah and Donna said just as Nick and Lisa pulled onto the grass.

"Hi, guys!" Dave yelled back, slightly confused.

Margaret ran out to Dave. "I invited everyone to Wildwood today. Forgot to tell you. So we have a lot of extra help before we head out, I guess?" she said as she playfully nudged him.

"I'll be right there, Greg. Give me a minute," Dave said as he turned to Margaret.

"If this market is going to be busy like this, I don't know how long we're going to be able to do the honor system. I'm just letting you know that right now. We may have to figure some things out," Dave said with a smile as he glanced at some more customers approaching the market.

Margaret paused and took a deep breath. "We're almost out of cucumbers and spaghetti squash. We may have to start outsourcing from local farmers if we want to keep everything in stock."

"And we might have to put in a gravel parking lot next to the market for parking. If it rains, this grass is going to turn into mud with all of the tire tracks," Dave said, watching more cars pull in.

A car pulled up the street, and someone yelled out the window.

Margaret and Dave both turned to see Bob, Margaret's father. "Where is my wife?"

Margaret laughed and rolled her eyes. "Inside the market, helping us. Why don't you park and come in for a bit?"

Bob shrugged. "That's why I'm here. Your mother told me to come help. Looks like you've got enough help, though. Is that my grandsons helping the lady with a crate of tomatoes?"

Margaret glanced over to see Michael opening the lady's trunk and Steven placing the box of tomatoes inside. "It is," she said, chuckling. "We're going to Wildwood to swim at the water park after this. Why don't you help and come with us?"

"Fine, but I'm only doing the lazy river," he said as he pulled his car onto the grass.

Dave glanced at Greg. "Oh, jeez. I've been keeping him waiting. I have to go get change at the bank. I'll be right back," he said, then gave Margaret a kiss on the cheek.

* * *

"What was it called again?" Susan asked as the retreat ladies left the Seahorse Inn that evening and started walking down Beach Avenue.

"The Sunny Seashell Inn is what Liam said. That's where the guys are staying," Kristen said as they eyed the signs in front of each home and inn that they passed.

"There it is on the corner," Darlene said, pointing.

Samantha stopped and stood on the sidewalk. "I don't know about this, girls. Were we invited? This feels weird."

"Samantha, we were invited by all of them. We're just hanging out. Nothing crazy," Tonya said as she pushed Samantha along.

They approached a tall green mansion with a huge porch with people hanging at tables, having drinks, and listening to a man play guitar and sing. On the grass, tons of chairs were set up with people lounging and relaxing.

"This is an inn?" Becky asked, flabbergasted.

"Oh, look. There's Ted." Maggie pointed.

The rest of the ladies made eyes at each other and chuckled. Besides Kristen and Liam, Maggie and Ted had seemed to hit it off, and everyone knew it.

"We saved you all seats over there," Ted said as he pointed to the side of the house where a ton of chairs sat around a firepit that was lit and smoking.

"Hey, ladies," Kyle, one of the guys in the group, said. "We'll show you the inside. They have a bar and restaurant, but there's a little window outside on the porch where you can order drinks and appetizers. They bring it right out to wherever you're sitting."

"I'm confused. Is this an inn with a restaurant and bar attached?" Tonya asked as they headed up the steps and inside.

"It is. Pretty neat, right?" Ted said.

They took a tour of the downstairs then got in line to order at the window.

Kristen and Liam stood next to each other at the end of the line. "I'm glad you came," Liam said with a smile.

"Of course I did. Don't be silly," Kristen said as she smiled back.

Chrissy stood in front of them with Samantha, and they both rolled their eyes and laughed.

After ordering drinks and heading back to the chairs by the

crackling firepit, they all breathed a sigh of relief as they relaxed and sipped their drinks.

"It's been quite the week," Ted said to everyone. "Very introspective. This is my first time ever doing something like this with a group of guys. My divorce is what prompted me to come, honestly. I needed something to clear my head."

"Same here," Susan said as she raised her glass.

"Cheers," the whole group said as they clinked glasses around the fire.

Kristen cleared her throat. "I'd like to say something, and I'm piggybacking off what Ted said. I think we've all been through something major in life recently, whether it's retirement, divorce, or grief. You name it. But what I've realized is that we all need to remember to take care of ourselves. If there's one thing I've learned during this week away with these wonderful women, it's that we all have our own story, and how we navigate that story is how we find happiness … and sometimes having some friends along for the ride makes it even easier to find."

"Couldn't have said it better," Tonya said as she took a sip of her drink.

Liam looked at Kristen adoringly from his chair. "Perfectly said."

Kristen smiled back. She didn't know what would happen between her and Liam after they went their separate ways the next day, but if it was meant to be, they'd find their way to each other again, that was for sure.

One of the workers at the inn approached them and stuck a few more logs into the firepit. It sent a plume of glittery gold flames into the air as he stoked the fire.

Everyone in the group grew quiet as they became entranced by the fire and soft crackling noises coming from it. Their time in Cape May was coming to an end, but it was the perfect evening surrounded by a new group of friends with memories to always hold on to.

EPILOGUE

"I can't believe it sold for that much," Margaret said as Dave drove his truck through Cape May.

"Me neither. I knew the bay house was going to sell above asking price with that bidding war, but not by *that* much," Dave said with a smile as he pulled the truck over on the one-way street in front of Howard's house. "This is it. This is the cottage I've fallen in love with."

Margaret glanced at the worn-down home then looked back at Dave. "Well, you said you wanted something you could use your building skills on."

"You don't seem excited about it," Dave said with a slight smile.

"I am, but I think I'll be more excited to see what updates you do to it," Margaret said as she opened the door and stepped out of the truck. "It's so funny how close this is to the Seahorse Inn," she said, glancing around to the backyard. "You said there's a private path to the beach through the back?"

"There is. I'll show you later on. First, I want you to meet Howard. I think his daughter is here too. She wants to meet us," Dave said as he led Margaret up the steps to the porch.

The front door opened before they could even knock. "Hi, there! I'm Callie, Howard's daughter. My dad told me about you. Come on in. By the way, that's my husband, Ryan, and our kids are out back playing," she said.

Dave and Margaret walked inside and immediately noticed Howard in the kitchen, making a sandwich. "I'll be right out. Just fixing lunch," Howard said as he put the mayonnaise jar back in the fridge.

"Well, I'm Dave. Nice to meet you," he said while shaking Ryan and Callie's hands. Margaret did the same.

"So, you want to buy our childhood home," Callie said as she started folding a laundry basket full of towels.

"Yes, that's the dream," Dave said as he put his arm around Margaret's shoulders.

"How do you feel about selling the home you grew up in?" Margaret asked.

Callie sighed. "I'm going to be honest. I hate the idea of it. Everywhere I look is a memory of something. I can't imagine this house not being in our family, but none of my siblings nor I want a second home, and plus, we don't live in New Jersey anymore. Dad is coming to live with us in Florida. That way we can keep an eye on him," she said with a wink.

"I heard that," Howard yelled from the kitchen as he sliced his sandwich in half.

"I totally get that. I bought my childhood home from my parents, and when Dave and I bought a bigger house together, I sold my childhood home to my cousin and her husband," Margaret said.

"Did Dad go over the price and all of that with you?" Callie asked as she looked over at Ryan.

"He did," Dave said.

"Well, alright then. I guess we'll get this sale moving forward then," Ryan said as he took the basket of folded towels up the stairs.

"Ryan is sick of dealing with this house. We come twice a

year to help my dad with any issues that arise, and let me tell you, there are many. I hope you're aware of that," Callie whispered.

"We are. I specifically wanted a house I could fix up," Dave said as he watched Howard walk into the room and sit down in a chair with his lunch.

"Dad, did you meet Dave's wife, Margaret?" Callie asked.

"Oh, no. I haven't. Nice to meet you," he said then took a bite of his sandwich.

Margaret smiled and waved. "Same to you."

"Oh, I wanted to show you two something upstairs before you leave. Follow me," Callie said as Margaret and Dave walked up the stairs behind her.

Callie stepped into a bedroom, then closed the door after Margaret and Dave walked in. "OK, I didn't have anything to show you, but I wanted to say this out of earshot of my father. Some neighbors a block away are trying to persuade him to let them buy the house. Ryan and I can't stand these people. They're not friendly, they trash their yard, keep their dog outside barking for hours and hours, and according to the neighbors next to them, have loud fights once a week. I do not want these people in my childhood home. My dad, on the other hand, doesn't know how to say no to people. So I'm going to get this sale sped up for you. You definitely want this house, right?"

"Yes," Margaret said before Dave could say anything.

Dave glanced at Margaret and smiled. "Yes, definitely."

* * *

Pick up book 16 in the Cape May Series, **Cape May Dreams,** to follow Margaret, Liz, Dave, and the rest of the bunch.

. . .

Start book 1 in my new Ocean City series, **A Summer in Ocean City.**

ABOUT THE AUTHOR

Claudia Vance is a writer of women's fiction and clean romance. She writes feel good reads that take you to places you'd like to visit with characters you'd want to get to know.

She lives with her boyfriend and two cats in a charming small town in New Jersey, not too far from the beautiful beach town of Cape May. She worked behind the scenes on television shows and film sets for many years, and she's an avid gardener and nature lover.

Made in the USA
Monee, IL
29 October 2024

68866278R00069